To Carrie
With bot ,
Marg.
24th May 2014

One Sun, One Moon,

Two Stars

by

Margaret Armand Smith

Bramley
PUBLISHING
HOUSE LIMITED

First published by AuthorHouse in November 2009
This edition published in 2011 by Bramley Publishing House Ltd

ISBN 978-0-9570566-0-2

Printed and bound in Great Britain by
CPI Group (UK) Ltd, Croydon, CR0 4YY

for my family

About the author

After working in a variety of jobs Margaret Armand Smith took a BA in English at Bath Spa University in her fifties. One Sun, One Moon, Two Stars is the first novel in her time travel trilogy.

Margaret has spent much of her life travelling – both when single and later with her husband and family. Now that their children have grown up Margaret and her husband live in Wiltshire with their four cocker spaniels.

margaretarmandsmith@hotmail.com

'We thank you for coming into our school. We enjoyed you
reading to us and answering our questions. ... we thoroughly
enjoyed [your visit] and your book...'

'...The tips you gave us were very helpful and inspired some of us
to be writers ourselves. Even though we will be in Secondary
school, we will all look out for your next book...'

'Thank you for answering my questions really well... I really
liked you reading the book...'

'... your tips were really useful, as I have always wanted to be an
author. I now have lots of ideas on how to improve my writing.
Furthermore you have inspired me to go home and write a
story...'

'... we enjoyed listening to you reading us some chapters in the
book, and we look forward to reading more of the story...'

'... when your new book comes out I'm DEFINITELY going to
buy it...'

'We all would like to say a big thank you for coming in and having
the time to answer our questions. We most enjoyed the story...
I can't forget to tell you even though I felt sick I did not want
to go home because I did not want to miss you coming to our
class.'

'... you are really good at reading your book and you are really
good at writing your books.'

Four signs to watch
Scattered first to last
Three travelled safely
The other
centuries set apart

'One Sun, One Moon,
Two Stars'

Chapter 1
The Rufus Stone

Who are they? Jonathan stared at the others sitting beside him on the rug. The boy had his long legs tucked under him and was eating his way through the plate of bread and butter. He glanced at the girl...Victoria... at least he'd remembered one of their names. She was quite pretty he decided, with her reddish ponytail dancing every time she moved her head. But it didn't stop him from wanting to know why they were here.

He'd given up his annual visit to his French grandparents to come to the New Forest with Sylvene. She'd never said anything about these two coming as well. Which is probably why he'd felt put out when the mini had driven into the farmyard and he'd seen them sitting in the back.

Jonathan rubbed his forehead. The niggling headache he'd had last night just before the thunderstorm was bothering him again. He looked up. Was there going to be another storm? The air felt heavy and oppressive enough, yet there wasn't a cloud in sight.

Yawning, he put down the book he'd been reading, propped himself on his left elbow and studied the others again. He usually got on with everyone so why was he so cross? Why did he resent them?

Get over it, he told himself, don't let it spoil the holiday. Determined to be pleasant he sat up, filled two mugs with tea and held one out to Victoria.

She smiled and put it on grass beside the rug. "Thanks," she said and turned away to watch a family of four heading for the car park.

Jonathan shrugged. So much for trying! Well if she didn't want to be friendly it was okay by him. He picked up 'The Camper's Guide to the New Forest' and stared blankly at the page.

Why *had* Sylvene invited them?

He looked across at her, curled up in the corner of a nearby bench sipping tea. She smiled at him then frowned. "Ben, do you want me to get some more bread?" she asked as the other boy reached for the last slice.

Ben! Of course! That was his name Jonathan thought, glad he hadn't had to ask.

"Mmm… nnm… thwanks," Ben spluttered.

Sylvene raised her eyes skywards. "What on earth was that supposed to mean?"

"I think – 'no thanks'," said Jonathan.

"Oh… that's a relief; but what about you two? You haven't eaten anything. I'm pretty certain I packed a box of muesli and there's still plenty of milk."

"No thanks," they chorused; then grinned at each other self-consciously.

"Sure?"

Victoria nodded. "Quite sure, honestly. I'm not hungry."

Sylvene glanced at her wristwatch. "In that case shall we make a start? Victoria, how about helping me with the picnic? Jonathan and Ben, could you do the washing up and then tidy the tent?"

"Where are we going for this picnic?" Ben asked sounding rather bored.

"I thought the Rufus Stone."

"Oh! Do we have to go there?"

"Why, what's wrong with the Rufus Stone?"

"Nothing! I'd just assumed you'd take us to the village."

"The vill... oh you mean East Oakhurst." Sylvene stood up. "No, I don't think so... at least not on our first day. But you needn't worry, we'll go there soon – I promise."

With a screech of its tyres the red mini reversed out of the parking spot scraping the next door car with its wing mirror. Jonathan fastened his seat belt and grinned at his companion in the back. "Her driving doesn't get any better, does it?"

Clutching the strap hanging down over the window as Sylvene drove out of the camp car park Ben shook his head. "No, worse if anything... Ouf..." he gasped and tightened his grip on the strap as the car leap-frogged the potholes pitting the mile or so of track between the campsite and the main road. It rumbled over a cattle grid and Sylvene slammed on the brakes. Wheels spinning on loose gravel the mini jerked to a stop in the entrance to the site.

3

All of them stared out of the windows. Streams of cars and buses charged towards them from every direction along the dual-carriageway. Sylvene put her foot down hard on the accelerator. The car shot forward, turned into a tiny gap and tagged on to the tail end of a long line of vehicles. Horn blaring, a black Mercedes roared by, the driver shaking his fist.

"Idiot!" She scowled and changed gear.

Jonathan grabbed the edge of his seat and leaned forward. "Where are we going?"

"Cadnam!" Sylvene wrenched at the steering wheel. The car swerved off the main road into a narrow lane. "Bother – now there's a pony and she's got a foal. I do wish they wouldn't wander aimlessly around the Forest."

"It is their home," said Victoria staring anxiously through the windscreen.

"Why Cadnam?" Jonathan asked when the mare and foal had been safely overtaken.

"Because…" Sylvene honked the horn at a small flock of sheep standing on the side of the road. They turned and ran into the scrub, tails whisking angrily. "Because it's where we turn off for the Rufus Stone."

"The rufus stone?" Victoria looked at her puzzled. "You mentioned that earlier… back at the camp. What exactly is a rufus stone?"

"Not *a… the* Rufus Stone," said Ben smugly. "It's a sort of monument. It's supposed to be the exact spot where William Rufus, the son of William the Conqueror, died. Though now-a-days some historians say it's not.

Anyway he was killed when hunting deer in the New Forest, allegedly by Sir Walter Tyrell."

"Oh… really!" Victoria sounded anything but interested. "I still don't see why we're making a special trip to see his monument."

"It's the first place most people *do* visit when they come to the forest," said Sylvene slowing down. "Bother! I missed the signpost. Did any of you see which way we have to go?"

"Left!" Victoria said looking back.

"And I thought you'd be interested," Sylvene continued as though her train of thought hadn't been interrupted. "It's a fascinating period of history…"

"Sylvene's such an archaeological freak, isn't she?" whispered Ben in Jonathan's ear.

Jonathan stared at the back of Sylvene's head, he'd never heard her mention archaeology.

"What's that, Ben? I wish you wouldn't mumble," she grumbled turning into a car park on the edge of a glade.

"Nothing," he said quickly.

"Hmm…" Sylvene sniffed loudly and switched off the engine. "You don't have to take my word for it. You can see people find this place intriguing. There are at least six coaches parked over there – one's even French – and I'm not going to begin to count the cars."

Sylvene wasn't exaggerating. There seemed to be hundreds of people milling around.

"It's a pity it's turned into such a lovely day," she murmured. "We could do with a good shower of rain.

Nothing dampens the day-trippers' enthusiasm like a good old English down-pour. It sends them running to the nearest tea-rooms."

Victoria squinted up at the clear blue sky. "Well you're going to be out of luck! There aren't even any clouds."

"Really... so what are those over there?"

"Okay... there are a few but look how far away they are and they're heading in the opposite direction."

Sylvene leaned back in her seat. "Why don't we wait and see?"

Jonathan sighed. Had it been such a good idea to come on this holiday? If all they were going to do was bicker and troop round to dreary monuments or boring archaeological sites, he might as well have gone to France. At least there he'd have met up with some of his cousins.

"Here comes the rain."

Jonathan blinked and stared out of the window. A moment ago the sun had been shining – now it was pouring.

As the first huge raindrops splattered the glass Sylvene looked at him in the mirror and smiled smugly. "See," she said. "What did I say? They don't like rain. Now we've got the place to ourselves. Shall we take a closer look at the Stone?"

"Oh – what a cheat. It's not even a stone." Jonathan stared indignantly at the triangular sheet of metal thrust deep into the ground.

"That doesn't matter." Sylvene's eyes glittered. "It's the atmosphere. The history! It's all around – in every tree, every brook, even in each blade of grass. Can't you feel it?"

He shook his head. "No!" he said baldly. "All I can feel is rain dripping down my neck. Can't we go back to the car?"

"Just a few more minutes," said Sylvene.

Disconsolate, Jonathan mooched up to the monument and began to read:

'Here stood the oak tree on which an arrow shot by Sir Walter Tyrell at a stag glanced and struck King William the Second, surnamed Rufus, on the breast of which he instantly died on the Second day of August 1100.'

"What's the date, Sylvene?"

"The second of August."

"BEN!"

Jonathan wheeled round. "What's he doing?"

Victoria pointed. "The idiot... he's carving something on that tree. It would serve him right if he got caught. Sylvene can't you..." her voice died away. She looked around, bewildered.

"What is it now?"

"Sylvene... she's gone!"

Chapter 2

The Hunt

Jonathan glanced around. It was true, Sylvene seemed to have vanished. He shook his head. "How odd… she was telling me about the Rufus Stone only a minute ago."

"Well, she's not here now," Victoria said sounding annoyed. "Ben, did you see where she went?"

"No." He scraped the blade of his penknife with his thumbnail, flicked a lump of bark into the air and glared at her. "I was busy." He snapped the knife shut and slipped it into the back pocket of his jeans. "She's probably taken off to the 'dig'."

"Without us?" Jonathan frowned.

Ben shrugged. "I told you she was an archaeological freak."

Victoria stared at him. "An archeological freak… Sylvene? Since when?"

"I dunno… always. In fact I wouldn't be surprised to learn that's why we've come to the New Forest. There's nothing she likes better than digging through layer after layer of dirt. She doesn't stop even if it starts pouring with rain. East Oakhurst is where she met my Dad."

"Your Dad?" Victoria looked at him.

Ben curled his lip. "Yes, my Dad. Do I have to repeat everything? He's Professor of Archaeology at Bristol

University and in charge of the excavations at East Oakhurst. Sylvene joined his team about three years ago… just after they found the remains of the Saxon village."

Victoria shook her head. "It's no good… I don't understand what all this has got to do with Sylvene disappearing."

"That's easy," Ben said. "She's done it before. She gets an idea into her head and that's the last you see of her for hours… sometimes even days. We could go and have a look…"

Victoria shook her head. "Leave here… no? That would be crazy. Suppose she came back? She wouldn't know where we'd gone."

"Victoria's right… it's not practical."

"Why not?" Ben stared at Jonathan. When there was no answer he rolled his eyes. "Okay, I get it… you two don't want to come. That's fine. It's up to you. But I'm going anyway." He walked across to a rough track zigzagging up the slope, hesitated and took a few steps back. "Are you quite sure you won't come?" he said flapping at a fly buzzing his head.

Jonathan glanced at Victoria. She shook her head. "Quite sure, thanks," he called. "We'll tell Sylvene where you've gone when she returns."

"When she returns… ha ha… very funny! Okay… but if you change your mind follow that path. We can't be more than a couple of miles from East Oakhurst."

Victoria stood quite still gazing down into the glade. By her reckoning a good half an hour had passed since Ben had left and there was still no sign of Sylvene. She looked down at Jonathan stretched out on the grassy slope and nudged him with her toe. "What are we going to do?"

"Do? Nothing!" He closed his eyes, enjoying the warmth of the sun on his face. "She'll turn up soon. She's got to – I'm starving and the picnic's in the car."

"But suppose she doesn't... come I mean?"

He opened his eyes and squinted at Victoria. "Then we'll have to go after Ben." He scowled. "And won't he crow? Oh, who cares... just relax. Try and look on the bright side."

"What bright side?"

"Well for one thing it's stopped raining."

"Oh!" Victoria peered up at the sky. "So it has. When did that happen?" She glanced across at the car park and her frown returned. "That's odd..."

"What now," said Jonathan?

"The coaches... they've all gone... I didn't see them leave... did you?"

"No. Does it matter?" He yawned. "Those sort of tours always have a pretty tight schedule, twenty minutes here, half an hour there. If we stay around long enough we're bound to see the next batch arrive."

"Perhaps... but Jonathan, I can't see any cars either."

He sat up. "No cars...you know what that means? Sylvene must have... hey... Victoria... wait..."

"Sorry… horses… coming this way," she called continuing to run down the slope.

"Horses? Are you sure? I can't hear anyt…oh!" Jonathan jumped up as the jingle of harness filled the air.

Victoria turned and grinned. "What do you call that… the wind in the trees?"

He smiled at her wryly. "Don't get too excited. It's probably only one horse…"

"I don't care how many there are. Horses mean people. Whoever's with them might be able to tell us how to get back to the camp."

"Back to the camp? I thought we said we'd go after Ben."

"No! You said that. I didn't," Victoria said stubbornly. "I'm fed up with hanging around waiting for those two. If I've got to walk a couple of miles I'm going back to the camp not somewhere I'd never heard of until today. At least there I can have a shower and something to eat. Sylvene brought loads of food with her… oh look… here they come…"

Waving her arms above her head she stepped into the middle of the path. The driver of the horse and cart that had just emerged from the trees stared at her then pulled his hood over his head, hunched his shoulders and whipped the horse into an unwilling canter driving it straight at Victoria.

"Victoria, look out." Horrified, Jonathan raced down the hill as, with a cry of alarm she flung herself off the path. Tailboard rattling and swaying from side to side, the cart careered past her, spitting a trail of dust and small pebbles into the air.

"Ouch!" Victoria dropped to her knees clasping her forehead with both hands. A trickle of blood oozed through her fingers.

"What happened... are you all right?"

She smiled wanly at Jonathan, her face white. "A stone... it's all right, I'm fine. But oh... it did hurt."

She held out her hands. He pulled her to her feet. "You're going to have an awful bruise," he said touching her forehead lightly.

She winced. "He wasn't very friendly was he?" she said as the cart disappeared into a line of firs at the top of the ridge.

"No... he wasn't," Jonathan said fiddling with the chain he wore that had got caught in the hair on the nape of his neck.

"Why do you think he didn't stop? We only wanted to ask the way."

"I've no idea. Just forget about it, it's not worth worrying about," Jonathan said softly. "Let's decide what we're going to do. Shall we go after Ben or back to the camp?"

"We could stay here. Wait for Sylvene to come back."

Jonathan shook his head. "I don't think there's any point. Surely if she was going to she'd have done it by now."

Victoria looked at him. "Then I guess we'd better go after Ben," she said reluctantly.

* * * * *

"I hope this *is* the way to East Oakhurst," said Jonathan walking slowly past a single oak tree by the side of the path.

Victoria shivered, her eyes wide and anxious. "Do you think Ben could be wrong?" Her voice shook a little.

Jonathan frowned. "Possibly. No wait a minute, that's rubbish. Don't listen to me. I've never been here before and he obviously has. So I guess he's probably right…"

"Yes, and as long as we don't leave this path we should be able to find our way back..." Victoria's voice trailed away.

Lost in their own thoughts they walked slowly along the track snaking up the side of the hill.

At the line of firs they hesitated, suddenly conscious of an eerie stillness. They looked back. The glade appeared unnaturally empty. Seeing the strain on Victoria's face Jonathan smiled reassuringly despite his own concerns.

A thick carpet of needles muffled their footsteps. The air was damp and chilly. When the firs began to thin out and were replaced by beech trees and oaks a dappled light fell across the track. Leaves rustled underfoot.

They'd been walking for sometime when a piercing screech stopped them in their tracks. Victoria clutched Jonathan. "What was that?" she whispered, her face pale.

He grinned with relief as a second screech broke the silence. "A pheasant," he said and they walked on, deeper into the wood.

The trees were now much larger and thicker, the light

dimmer. Silence dominated their surroundings broken only by an occasional call of a bird flitting from tree to tree.

Away in the distance came a harsh cry.

Jonathan turned to Victoria. "Did you hear that?"

She nodded.

"It sounded like a hunting horn but I don't see how it can be… it's the wrong time of year." Frowning, he walked on.

Victoria followed a little way behind.

When light began to filter through the canopy of leaves again Jonathan glanced upwards. "We must be coming out," he said, relieved.

Victoria grinned idiotically at his back. "Thank goodness…"

"Ssh!"

She bit her lip and waited.

"Hounds," Jonathan said. "I can hear hounds baying… nearby." He turned and grabbed her arm almost jerking her off her feet.

Side by side they raced towards an opening ahead. Together they flew out of the shadows into the sunshine and skidded to a stop.

For as far as they could see a carpet of purple heather spread across the Forest, broken only by an occasional copse of trees and patches of gorse. A string of hillocks drew their gaze to the horizon.

A second cry from the hunting horn broke the spell. They leaned over the edge of the ridge and peered into the valley below. A group of horsemen was circling a tangle of brambles, beating the flaps of their saddles with the handles of their whips. Hounds milled between the horses' legs, whining noisily. One huntsman cracked his whip urging the pack into the undergrowth.

Almost immediately a stag broke cover.

Two riders spurred their horses forward forcing the terrified animal further into the open. At full gallop, the deer raced along the valley, horses and riders on either side, hounds in full cry. Suddenly it darted to the right, leapt a fallen tree, and raced across the open heathland hotly pursued by baying hounds.

Before long all that remained of the hunt and its quarry was a thin ribbon of dust floating slowly upwards.

"I'm sure something *is* wrong," Jonathan whispered.

"Wrong… What do you mean? Why do you think something's wrong?"

"The hunt… it's only just August and they're hunting…"

"Does it matter?"

"August…" He shook his head. "No… forget it. Let's get going. At this rate we're never going to reach East Oakhurst."

"How long have you lived on a farm?" asked Victoria as they walked slowly down the side of the hill?

"All my life. Where do you live?"

"London. I'd like to live in the country but my Dad's work is in London." She tilted her head and slowed a little. "Jonathan is it my imagination, or can I hear running water?"

Jonathan smiled slowly. "Well, if it isn't running water, I'm imagining it as well. Look down there…"

Victoria followed the line of his arm. On the bottom of the valley floor the sun glinted on sprays of water bubbling out from under a huge boulder. She licked her lips.

Jonathan grinned. "You're thinking what I'm thinking!"

She grinned back and nodded. Together they leapt off the track, skidded down the side of the hill on their bottoms and landed in a giggling, tangled heap by the mouth of a stream. Lying on their stomachs they sucked up mouthfuls of the delicious, icy water trickling over a bed of pebbles.

"That was so good." Victoria sat up and fastened the band around her ponytail more securely. "I hadn't realised how thirsty I was." Jonathan rolled on to his back and she giggled. "Your t-shirt's covered in mud."

Jonathan laughed. "You can't talk. So's yours… are you ready?"

She nodded.

"Good, let's get on then."

"You know this is the longest two miles I've ever walked," Victoria complained. "It's hours since we left the Rufus Stone." She glanced at her wrist. "How strange… my watch says twelve o'clock. It can't possibly be. It was twelve o'clock when we got to the car park. What time do you make it?"

"It's… that's odd… mine says twelve o'clock as well." Jonathan tapped the face of his watch.

The track had now become a man-made barrier between open heathland and a river. On the far side of the river was a field of waist-high corn.

Jonathan stared. A line of men were walking across the field cutting the corn… with scythes! "Victoria…" he gasped.

"What?"

"I'm… er… beginning to think something really odd has happened…"

"It doesn't matter." She pointed. "Over there… houses." She broke into a trot, burbling happily. "Ben must have known what he was talking about but I think he was wrong about the distance – it was more like four miles than two – don't you think?"

"Yesss…" Jonathan stared at the row of low thatched roofs nestling beneath the hill at the edge of the corn field. "*If* this is East Oakhurst."

Victoria stumbled and shot him a startled glance. "What?"

"I'll explain later," he said stepping on to a rickety bridge.

But as they headed along what was obviously the main street he became more and more convinced that this wasn't an ordinary village. The houses, if you could call them houses, were squalid. Some needed the roofs re-thatching, others had gaping holes in their walls.

Surely no one could actually live in them?

He jumped as Victoria brushed against him. "You know this place is creepy," she whispered. "Where is everyone? I don't think I like it here…" A loud shout broke the silence. Relief flooded into her eyes and she pointed: "Voices – over there."

Running swiftly they rounded a corner and stopped. Six or seven men were walking around the churchyard scything the grass.

"Let's ask them the way to the 'dig'," said Jonathan pushing open the gate.

But before they could enter the churchyard a tall figure marched down the path towards them calling: "Qui êtes vous?"

Chapter 3
East Oakhurst

French?

Jonathan stared. His initial thought had been that the men must be tourists – until he'd noticed their clothes. Tourists wore jeans, t-shirts and flip-flops; not tunics, tights and cloaks. Anyway, that was stupid. Who'd ever heard of gangs of French tourists cleaning up random English churchyards?

"Is he saying what I think he's saying?"

Jonathan nodded. "He wants to know who we are."

"That's what I thought. Why? What's it to do with him? And why the French? Ask him about the dig? No… on second thoughts I think I'll do it," and with that Victoria pushed past Jonathan.

Two men stepped sideways, blocking her way.

"Bonjour." She smiled at them confidently.

They stared back, their expressions impassive.

"Could you tell us how we get to the archaeological site?" She wrinkled her nose. French had never been her favourite language. "We think two of our friends might be there."

The men continued to stare, silently.

The young man tapped the side of his leather boots with the handle of a whip. He gazed at Jonathan thoughtfully. "Why are you here?" he said ignoring Victoria.

She flushed. "There's no need to be rude. If you can't tell us the way to the dig it doesn't matter. We'll just go and find someone who can…"

"She's right," Jonathan interrupted calmly. "We're looking for our friends."

The man standing behind the speaker leaned forward and whispered something in his ear. He nodded, his eyes never leaving Jonathan's face. "I am told that the Bailiff returned from Linhest with someone in the cart."

"Ben… it's got to be Ben," Jonathan muttered.

"Why Ben? Why not Sylvene?"

Jonathan glanced at Victoria and shrugged. "I suppose it could be her… but I think it's unlikely."

Victoria scowled. "Well, I hope it is; that's all I've got to say. She's got an awful lot of explaining to do."

"Yes, she has." Jonathan lowered his voice to make sure none of the men could hear. "I've got loads of questions for her."

The young man rubbed his chin. The others hovered anxiously. "I will take these travellers to the hall," he said at last. "Stephen!" A short man, not much taller than Victoria, pushed his way out of the crowd. "Take charge here. When everything is finished come and find me. There are many things to be done before the wedding."

"Travellers!" exclaimed Victoria her face reddening with indignation.

Jonathan shot her a warning glance. She glared at him – but remained silent.

"But Master Robert, there are two of them. Should

not one of us go with you?" Stephen said.

"What?" Victoria almost spat out the word. "What is the idiot talking about now? He thinks we're going to attack 'Master Robert', doesn't he…?"

"Ssh!" Jonathan frowned. "They're trying to hear what you're saying."

"So what? Would they understand? I don't think so. Have you heard any of them speak English?" Her eyes widened as Robert pulled a dagger from his belt. "Now what's he doing?"

Robert felt the tip of the blade. "There is no need for anyone to accompany me," he said, smiling. "Not while I have this and my whip."

"Even so," said one of the men.

"Even so," Victoria mimicked under her breath.

"Master Robert… Master Robert."

The wheezy shout startled Jonathan and Victoria. Both whirled around. Stumbling up the path was a stout man.

"What is it, Samuel Goodchilde?" Robert called walking to meet him.

His breath coming in painful gasps, Samuel stopped and removed his cap. He bowed low, then mopped his forehead. "T'is the Gleeman, Master Robert… the Gleeman is come. Your father sent me to fetch you back to the hall. They are discussing the music for Lady Adela's wedding."

"The Gleeman!" Robert beamed and thrust the dagger back in its sheath. "Why, you bring me excellent news. Now all the entertainers are here. Samuel, you

21

are in good time. It was my intention to take these two strangers to my father, but…" for an instant Jonathan thought he saw a hint of laughter lurking in the young man's eyes, "…Luke Perkins declared they could be dangerous. Now you are here you can be my guard." He clapped him on the back, turned and beckoned to Jonathan and Victoria. "Follow me."

Without waiting to check they were obeying he marched from the churchyard, his cloak billowing behind.

"Friendly lot, aren't they?" muttered Victoria out of the side of her mouth before starting after him.

Jonathan scowled. From the moment they'd arrived in the village he'd been trying to make some kind of sense of everything he'd seen and heard. Now he had an answer – but it was an answer he didn't want to believe.

He stared after the two figures crossing the street. They should leave – *immediately* – with or without Ben; but Victoria wouldn't like it. He didn't like it. But what else could… A savage blow caught him between the shoulder blades. He staggered.

"Move, lad… don't yer keep Master Robert waiting."

Jonathan stared at the thin-faced man who'd struck him. Although he was grinning his eyes were cold and hard. Jonathan clenched his fists and raised them.

The man reached out, caught his right wrist and twisted it behind his back. "Didn't you hear?" he hissed. "I said *move*."

Two more men moved closer but before they could do anything Samuel Goodchilde stepped up to Jonathan and rested his hand on his shoulder. "I'd do what he says, lad."

Jonathan stared at him defiantly.

"Please yerself… but *I'd* do what he says." Samuel winked at the man holding Jonathan who immediately released his wrist. "Right… let's go. Jest make sure you keep close to me and everyfink'll be alright."

As Jonathan followed the older man down the steps his eyes strayed towards the river. There was no way he could leave now – alone.

At the end of the street Samuel slowed and pointed. A path was winding its way up the hillside at the back of the village. A forbidding fence dominated the skyline. "That's where we're going lad. Best hurry. We dun want ter keep Master Robert waiting."

Jonathan's heart sank. He sighed and followed his companion up the hill.

The two gates creaked noisily as they swung slowly open.

"I suppose we've got to go in," Victoria whispered, a muscle twitching nervously at the side of her jaw.

Jonathan nodded unwillingly. They walked slowly into the compound.

"What is this place?" Victoria said, her voice husky with fear.

Any hopes Jonathan might have been clinging to, vanished. The courtyard was almost the size of a football pitch. Barns lined three sides, some large, some small. What was most noticeable was that all these buildings were in good repair.

A single large building over-looked the hovels in the valley on the remaining side. Smoke spewed through a hole in its roof. Nearby a cluster of smaller huts stood in its shadow.

They were nearly in the centre of the compound when a horse nickered. Jonathan and Victoria looked back. A bay mare was trotting towards them. As it went past the rider glanced at Victoria, his lip curling unpleasantly.

"The stables," Jonathan said quietly as the man dismounted by the doorway of a long low building and led the horse inside.

She rubbed her eyes, wearily. "I don't care what it is. I just want to get out of here. This place gives me the creeps. As soon as we find the others I vote we leave."

"Er… that might be… damn, here he comes again," said Jonathan.

Robert nodded at Samuel Goodchilde. "Stay here. I will go and see what the Bailiff wants."

The Bailiff… he was the person who'd come back with someone in his cart. Victoria stared curiously as the two men paced backwards and forward over the cobblestones, deep in conversation. "What do you think they're talking about?"

"I wish I knew," Jonathan said. He frowned. There was something unpleasantly familiar about the Bailiff. Where had he seen him before? He was about to ask

Victoria if she knew when he caught sight of a movement out of the corner of his eye. He edged over to one of the barns and peered inside. Three men were beating a pile of corn with heavy wooden sticks.

"Ere… where do ya think yer going?"

Jonathan jumped.

Samuel Goodchilde was standing beside him.

"Nowhere… I wasn't going anywhere! I wond… *what* are they doing?"

The man burst out laughing. "Never seen anyone use a flail before, boy? 'Ow else does ya think they thresh the corn?"

Thresh the corn!

Finally, here was the proof he needed. No one in the twenty-first century threshed corn like that… at least not in England. Jonathan shivered. The farmers he knew either hired contractors to bring in the harvest or did it themselves driving huge combine harvesters complete with computer software.

He watched the men working, oblivious to his surroundings.

"Jonathan, I'm getting the weirdest feeling," Victoria said joining them by the open door.

"So am I," he said grimly. "In fact there's something I need to tell…"

"Oi – you two… in here". The Bailiff and Robert were standing in the stable doorway.

The smell of warm horseflesh took Jonathan by surprise. A picture of his little sister galloping across their fields on her pony flashed into his mind. His throat tightened. When would he see her again? He swallowed. Would he ever see her again?

They walked past a tethered horse lipping at the hay in a manger and stopped by the Bailiff who grinned; but his eyes were still cold and calculating.

Victoria smiled at him warily.

"Come closer." The man beckoned again. "There is something you should see." He tossed aside a pile of sacking in the back of a nearby cart.

"Ohhh…!" Victoria screamed. She hurled herself forward. "What have you done to him…?" she yelled.

Chapter 4

Accusations

"So you *do* know him." A complacent grin almost split the bailiff's face in half. He rubbed his massive hands together.

"Of course… he's our friend," Victoria snapped. She helped lift Ben into a sitting position and caught her breath. "His hands are tied together."

"Yes. He tried to attack me." The Bailiff looked faintly amused at her struggles with the twine around Ben's wrists.

"No I didn't," Ben protested weakly.

Victoria winced and looked away. His face was a mess. Blood oozed from a cut on his lower lip. His left eye had almost vanished beneath a mass of purple bruising; the other was just a narrow slit.

A wave of cold fury swept over Jonathan. Why would anyone attack a complete stranger in that way? He clenched his fists but before he could move or say anything a slim figure emerged from the shadows.

"Was it necessary to beat the boy so badly?" Robert asked, his voice very quiet.

"Why yes Master Robert. Didn't you hear? He attacked me."

"I know. That is what you told me earlier. Yet I see

no marks on your face. Nor have you explained why he assaulted you."

"I told you – because I caught him setting snares in the Forest," the Bailiff blustered.

Jonathan tensed. "Setting snares… that's a lie. We don't have any snares. Ben was coming here. In fact we were going after him when you drove by."

"What?" Victoria flung the length of twine to the ground. She grabbed Jonathan's arm and shook it. "What did you say?"

Ben rubbed the marks on his wrists. "Thanks," he mumbled.

"That's all right," she said, her eyes still fixed on Jonathan. "Come on… what do you mean – *'drove by'?*"

"Remember the horse and cart… the one that nearly knocked you down?"

"Of course – the man was a pig."

"Meet the 'pig'." Jonathan pointed at the Bailiff.

"Him?" Victoria glared at the Bailiff and stamped her foot. She turned to Robert. "Jonathan's right… he's lying. He couldn't have caught Ben poaching. Where are these snares? Search me if you like. If Ben's a poacher we must be too." And she threw out her arms dramatically.

"What proof have you that I am lying?" snarled the Bailiff. "It is your word – against mine."

Robert frowned. "Enough! We will go and find my father. He will know what to do. But I tell you this now,

Bailiff, you should not have attacked the boy in that way."

"But Master Robert…"

"I said – enough," Robert repeated angrily, making for the door.

"Careful." Jonathan leapt into the cart and grabbed Ben as he stood and wobbled dangerously. "Here, let me help. Sit on the end of the cart. That's right. Now swing your legs over… careful… don't hurry… take your time." With Jonathan's help, Ben got his legs over the side of the cart.

"Are you ready?" Jonathan said, holding him steady.

"I think so."

"Good. Victoria, get ready to grab him. Go Ben!"

Ben slid to the ground.

Grinning, Jonathan jumped out of the cart. "Well done. Can you walk?"

"I… er… think so," said Ben swaying a little.

"Then perhaps we'd better go after Robert."

"Wait… just a minute… before we go there's something I need to know." Ben grabbed Jonathan's arm. "What was all that about – just now – poaching and the rest of it?"

Jonathan hesitated. He'd have to tell him – but this wasn't the right time. It was more important to get away while there was still a chance. He shook his head. "Poaching was… is… a very serious offence… Don't worry about it. We'll explain later I promise."

"Oh no you don't … not later… now! I want to know why he lied."

Victoria examined her fingernails. "Perhaps he thought it would make him look important," she said and nibbled at the jagged edge of a nail torn while she'd struggled with the ropes around his wrists.

"He must be mad! Why would I want to poach anything? Anyway, that's not the point. Even if I was a poacher it still wouldn't give him the right to hit me like that. If you won't tell me I'll find a policeman." Ben hobbled towards the open door.

Jonathan resisted calling him back. "You know something; I think he's going to find that difficult," he said.

"Impossible, I'd say."

Jonathan stiffened. He hadn't realised he'd spoken out loud.

Victoria smiled at him. "It's all right... there's no need to look like that. I'm not an idiot. I didn't want to believe it at first – but then who would? Still, I'm beginning to get used to the idea."

Jonathan sighed. "Are you? I wish I could say the same. Mind you, it's a relief knowing I can at least stop worrying about how to tell you. All we have to do now is tell Ben. I wondered if..." He broke off seeing Victoria's face. "What is it?"

"Nothing. I was just trying to imagine Ben's reaction when we tell him we've gone..."

"Oi – you two."

Startled, they spun round. Samuel Goodchilde was in the doorway, his burly figure blocking out most of the light… escape was impossible.

Unconsciously Victoria drew closer to Jonathan. "What do you want?"

"Nothing… Master Robert sent me. 'E wants yer in the Hall – now."

They glanced at each other then, without speaking, followed him from the stables and across the compound. At the front door of the Hall he stopped, his hand on the latch. "Now before we go in just listen ter wot I 'ave to say. Yer friend is inside. Wait with 'im 'til I calls yer," he said and pushed open the door.

Jonathan nodded, took Victoria's hand, led her into the room… and gasped.

In front of them was a room that was like nothing they'd ever seen before. It was large, so large it was more like a school assembly hall than someone's house.

The windows had been covered by strips of sacking. The only light came from a row of flaming torches fixed to the north wall. Up in the roof a line of oak beams supported the thatch.

It was sparsely furnished, a single trestle table with benches on either side in the centre and, at the far end, a second, more ornate table on a raised dais flanked by eight high-backed chairs.

Victoria nudged Jonathan. "It's like a film set, isn't it?" she whispered. "I can just see Robin Hood fighting his way out of here."

"Hmm… I wish I could… where's Ben?"

"Over there." Victoria pointed at a figure slumped

across the trestle table. She started forward.

Jonathan caught her arm. "Where do you think you're going?" he hissed.

"To see if he's okay, of course."

"Well don't. Where did that man go?"

"Which man?"

"The one that brought us here."

"Oh him. Over there, by the fire. He's talking to Robert."

Perhaps he should pinch himself, Jonathan thought glancing around. It was hard to believe they were standing in a medieval hall watching a group of men huddled around a fire actually lit beneath a hole in the roof. He rubbed his eyes which were beginning to smart in the smoke-filled atmosphere and peered through the haze. One of the men was turning a pig on a spit; a second was playing a flute. The rest stood in a semi-circle around Robert and Samuel Goodchilde listening to their conversation.

"I wish I could hear what those two were talking about," Jonathan murmured as the two men looked their way.

"I wish they'd stop staring. They're making me nervous," said Victoria. She gasped suddenly and pointed. The tapestry behind the high table had moved.

Jonathan drew in his breath as a hidden door opened and two more men came into the room. He didn't recognise the taller one but the other he knew only too well – the Bailiff.

As they walked past the trestle table Ben lifted his

head. Anger and fear flashed across his face.

Jonathan nudged Victoria.

"What?" she said her eyes fixed on the approaching men.

"I think we need to get closer to Robert."

"Why? What about Ben?"

"Leave him where he is. We can keep an eye on him but this is really important. I want to find out what's going on."

Victoria threw an anxious glance at Ben. "But he looks so ill."

"He'll be all right," Jonathan said coldly.

"Why are you so mad at him? What's he done?"

"What's he done? If it wasn't for him we wouldn't be in this mess now."

"You can't know that?"

Jonathan raised his eyebrows incredulously. "I'm not going to argue," he snapped and walked away.

"Are these your travellers, Robert?"

"They are, Father. The third is seated over there."

Sir Henry turned and looked across at Ben. "You… come here."

Ben glanced up.

"Yes, you lad," Sir Henry said impatiently.

Ben got up and walked slowly towards the little group, his expression wary.

Sir Henry frowned. "Who hit you?"

"The Bailiff, Father," Robert said quickly. "He claims

he caught him poaching. But the boy denies it."

"Poachers usually do," his father said dryly.

"Ben doesn't tell lies."

Robert's father raised an eyebrow surprised at the unexpected interruption.

Victoria flushed. "It's true," she added defiantly.

Jonathan caught her arm. "My sister is right," he said.

Victoria gasped: "Wha…?"

Jonathan frowned, shook his head and hurried on before she could say anything else, "Our brother is no poacher."

"That's not what the Bailiff says."

"I don't care what he says. I know he couldn't have found him setting snares because we haven't any to set."

Sir Henry frowned.

Jonathan held his breath and waited.

"If you weren't poaching why were you in the Forest?"

"Sir Henry…"

"Silence Bailiff. Let the lad answer."

Jonathan swallowed. "My name is Jonathan, sire. My sister is called Victoria, my brother – Ben. Our Father died at Michaelmas…"

Ben spluttered and stared at him.

"Died? How?" demanded the Bailiff?

"An accident, sir." Jonathan glared at Ben, daring him to interrupt again. "Our poor Mother is unable to work – because of the babes – so it was agreed we three should leave home and seek employment."

Victoria choked and buried her face in her hands.

Pretending to look sympathetic, Jonathan put his arms around her and pulled her close. "You're going to give us away," he hissed in her ear.

Victoria gulped. "Sorry," she whispered her shoulders shaking.

"We were fortunate, sire," Jonathan continued, letting her go. "The day we left home we met with a troupe of travelling players…"

"Of course! That explains your clothes," Robert said and grinned.

Jonathan bowed.

"I don't care what he says, there weren't any players in the Forest when I came across him…" the Bailiff jerked his thumb at Ben.

"Of course there weren't… they'd already left."

"The players left you in the Forest?" exclaimed Robert.

Jonathan nodded. "Yes, but I do not blame them." He stepped on Victoria's foot as her shoulders began to shake again.

"Ooh…!" She clapped a hand to her mouth.

"Sadly sire," Jonathan said looking directly at Sir Henry, "we quickly discovered our talents do not lie in tumbling or singing. Nor have any of us learned to play a musical instrument. Shortly after the troupe left Lyndhurst the leader told us he no longer needed our help and suggested we part company. He advised us to

35

go – preferably in the opposite direction to them."

Using Sir Henry's laughter as cover, Ben edged sideways. "Has he gone completely mad?" he whispered, sidling up to Victoria.

"Ssh! Don't set me off again. We'll explain later."

Sir Henry shook his head but his expression was much less severe.

They all waited anxiously.

"Hmm," he said at last, "my Lady has been complaining about the extra work the marriage of our daughter is creating. The girl could help her. No doubt Conrad could make good use of that lad." He pointed at Jonathan. "That leaves the other one." He stroked his neat beard reflectively. "Bailiff?"

"Yes my Lord?"

"Does the miller need help with the harvest?"

The Bailiff's eyes lit up. "Oh yes my Lord."

"Good. Then he can work at the mill. Robert you can take him there in the morning. But for now…"

"Yes Father?"

"Find more suitable clothes for them in place of these…" he flicked his fingers contemptuously at Jonathan's jeans "…these costumes. Your mother would be shocked to see the wench dressed in that way."

Chapter 5
High Table, Low Table

"I don't understand."

Jonathan and Victoria eyed Ben uneasily. They were sitting on a tree trunk that had been dumped in a corner of the compound. He was pacing up and down, too wound up to sit still.

He stopped right in front of them, running his hands through his hair, his face pale and streaked with dirt. "Can't we leave now? I'm afraid if we stay here someone else might try to beat me up. I know one thing… as soon as I get a signal on my mobile I'm ringing my Dad."

"Have you still got your mobile?" Jonathan asked twisting the chain around his neck.

"Yes," Ben said shortly.

"And it doesn't work?"

Ben shook his head. "I told you – no signal."

"I see. Do you really want to go back to the camp?" said Jonathan

"Of course, but we should go by Lyndhurst! If you remember," Ben said his voice heavy with sarcasm, "I want to make a complaint. There might not be a police station here but I know there's one in Lyndhurst."

"Robert told us to wait here until we heard the evening meal bell," said Victoria bending over to draw a picture in the dust with her finger.

"That's an even better reason for leaving. I'm not interested in 'living-history' projects, particularly when taken to extremes... like they obviously have here. I mean fancy speaking French all the time... and what was going on back in there?" Ben pointed at the Hall.

"What do you mean?" said Victoria.

"Jonathan going on about us being brothers and sisters; that man saying jeans were fancy dress. This is fancy dress." Ben tugged the sleeve of his tunic. His eyes narrowed and he glared at Jonathan and Victoria. "Come on... you two know something I don't know – I can feel it. Tell me."

"Sit down and we'll explain," said Victoria putting the finishing touches to a new moon she'd drawn.

"I don't want to... just tell me."

Avoiding Ben's eyes, Jonathan reached for a stalk of straw swirling around in the dust. "It's quite simple," he said searching for the right words. He crushed the empty ears of corn between his thumb and fore-finger. "We've gone back in time."

Ben gaped. "We've what... no... that's ridiculous. You're making it up."

"He's not." Victoria rubbed out the moon and started again. "He's just not making a very good job of explaining."

"That's not fair," Jonathan protested, "how much clearer does *we've gone back in time* have to be?"

"Okay, okay, I see what you mean." Ben smiled

condescendingly. "Don't worry Jonathan. I had already realised that we've got caught up in one of those '*living-history*' projects. I expect Dad arranged it. He sets them up all over the country."

"That's not what I said!" Jonathan said indignantly.

"No, it isn't," Victoria agreed.

Ben curled his lip. "Aw… come on!"

"Why don't you shut up and listen?" snapped Jonathan. "I'll say this once more… in words of one syllable… *we have gone back in time*. Do you understand? Is that plain enough?"

"I understand all right. I understand you think I'm a complete idiot."

"Yes!"

Ben blinked. "And what's that supposed to mean?"

"It's simple. Since we met you've done nothing to convince me you're not an idiot. In fact I'd say the opposite. You haven't listened to anything we've said or done anything we've suggested. You do your own thing all the time – and look where that got you… accused of being a poacher and getting beaten up."

Ben's angry glare was slowly replaced by a faintly patronising look. He pulled his mobile phone out from under his belt and began tapping some numbers. "Nothing… This must be a really bad reception area. Okay… so sometimes I get carried away... I like doing my 'own thing' as you call it. But Jonathan – you don't need to be embarrassed. It's an easy mistake to make. These sort of places always feel a little odd until you get used to them."

"Ben – this is not a '*living-history*' project. Your mobile phone will not work because we have gone back in time."

"Oh for goodness sake… I wish you'd stop saying that. If you're so sure tell me this – exactly what century are we in?"

The glint in Jonathan's eyes faded a little. He smiled… a rueful smile… and shook his head. "Do you know I don't have any idea?" He looked around, searching for inspiration, "er… it could be Norman."

"Norman?" Ben dropped the phone and sat down hurriedly a variety of expressions flitting across his face.

Puzzled, Jonathan and Victoria glanced at each other.

Shivering, Ben rubbed the marks around his wrist. "That might be the explanation…"

"Explanation for what?" Victoria asked when he stopped in mid-sentence.

He blinked, nervously. "Why there aren't any cars! And the roads… they're not really roads are they? They're more like muddy tracks. I should have worked it out. After all, I'm the one who's been here before. It's been staring me in the face but I didn't see. I guess I didn't want to see."

"See what?" said Victoria.

"Oh, loads of things… those dirty little shacks in the village for one – and then there's the French for another..."

"Are you saying you believe us?" asked Jonathan.

Ben grinned. "You know, I think I must be," he said his confidence returning.

Victoria caught her breath. "Oh, thank goodness! So what should we do?"

"Do? I don't know." Ben wrinkled his nose. "I know one thing though, I'd like to find out why we've gone back." He stared at them expectantly.

There was a tense silence.

"Haven't you worked that out either?" he challenged.

Victoria opened her mouth, closed it and shook her head.

Jonathan frowned. "No," he admitted reluctantly. "But you're right. There has to be a reason."

That night Jonathan lay on his back and stared into the darkness. Except for an occasional snore the room was quiet. So why couldn't he sleep?

He closed his eyes and Ben's question popped into his mind again. Why *had* they gone back in time? The trouble was however hard he tried he couldn't think of an answer – at least not one that made any sense.

Behind him some rushes rustled, breaking the stillness for a moment. It stopped as quickly as it had begun. Silence fell over the room again. It wasn't fair, Jonathan thought, wriggling around in the dirt trying to get comfortable. Why was he the only one who couldn't sleep?

Another soft rustle… this time to his left. Jonathan stiffened. Someone else must be awake. Propping himself on his elbow he peered into the darkness just as a stream of sparks flew out of the dying fire, popping and crackling. A figure was bending over the embers pushing them together. He drew in his breath sharply. The man straightened up and looked his way before melting into the shadows.

Jonathan rubbed his eyes. It had all happened so quickly for a moment he thought he'd been dreaming. Then a soft strain filled the air. He smiled faintly and wrapped the rather smelly cloak that Robert had given him with the tunic tightly around his body and lay down again. Cushioning his head in his hands he relaxed and let the music wash over him.

What a weird finish this was to a really weird day, he thought. Mind you, the weirdest part had been the moment the evening bell began ringing.

Before the peals had died away the gates had flown open and what seemed like hundreds of people streamed into the compound. For a moment he'd thought they were going to be separated, flung in every direction by a growing horde stampeding towards the Hall.

Luckily, Victoria had had the sense to grab his cloak while he'd yelled at Ben to stay close, at least as close as possible.

With the ring of wooden clogs on cobblestones in their ears, they'd been pushed and jostled across the yard, the centre of an unyielding, swirling mass. Once Jonathan had caught a glimpse of Ben's mobile being trampled underfoot then it had disappeared again in the relentless drive forward. A final surge from behind had sent them sprawling across the threshold of the Hall.

Most of the crowd had been too busy searching for a place at the lower table to worry about the three strangers slithering across the floor on their knees. Embarrassed, they'd scrambled to their feet, found three seats reasonably close together and sat looking around curiously at their surroundings.

A crisp linen cloth had been thrown over the High Table where Sir Henry and Lady Faversham sat with Robert and a young woman on their right and the Bailiff and Priest on their left. White napkins nestled by pewter plates. Silver goblets glinted in the soft light from the three simple candelabra spaced evenly along the table.

It was all very different to the bare lower table where they were sitting.

When the door behind the High Table had opened a single file of servants entered the room. Some had presented their trays, laden with steaming fish, roast meats and vegetables, to Sir Henry. The rest had made for the lower table.

Jonathan had clutched his stomach trying to stop it rumbling. He'd glanced around, self-consciously.

"Hungry, lad?" His neighbour had nudged him, grinning.

He'd nodded. Breakfast had been a long time ago and all he'd had then was a cup of tea.

"Won't be long," the man had said eyeing the servants moving their way ladling dollops of lumpy grey stew on to thick slices of bread.

Despite being hungry Jonathan had waited before starting, wondering how he was meant to eat the meal. He had quickly realised that although a few of his neighbours had their own knife or spoon kept in the leather pouches tied to their belts everyone else just used their fingers.

In the darkness Jonathan licked his lips remembering that first mouthful! Despite the off-putting colour the gravy had been delicious. He'd eaten quickly, every crumb, every drop. But he had still been hungry when the last mouthful had been swallowed so had picked up the soggy, slice of bread.

"Put it down."

"Put what down?"

"The bread, idiot."

"What? Why?" Surprised at the vehemence in Ben's voice, Jonathan had peered at him around the back of the man sitting between them.

"It's bad manners to eat the trencher."

"The what?"

"Trencher – that slice of bread is a trencher. Now what's wrong?" Ben had added belligerently seeing him stare.

"Nothing... nothing's wrong. I was just wondering how you knew it was called a trencher, that's all. I've never heard of them."

"Why should you? I wouldn't have either if it weren't for Dad. It's a pity he's not here. He'd have loved this place. Norman England's easily his favourite period of history."

Jonathan winced. That was something else he'd

forgotten. Ben had told them earlier that his father was Professor of Archaeology at Bristol University. The music quickened and he closed his eyes. How the people had danced after the evening meal, their faces eager, their laughter filling the hall. How long had the dancing lasted?

He couldn't remember – but it didn't matter.

What he did remember was that once the music had stopped Sir Henry had stood up and the laughter had died away. As the party from the High Table left, the now silent men and women had bowed or curtseyed before following them from the room until only a small group of young men were left with Jonathan, Ben and Victoria.

It had seemed quite natural to Jonathan that Victoria would stay with them. But when a servant girl had returned and offered to take her to the women's quarters Ben had insisted she go.

"Be sensible," he had said. *"If you stay somebody's bound to tell the Bailiff."*

Victoria had turned unhappily to Jonathan. *"What do you think?"*

He had wanted to say: *"It doesn't matter. Stay with us."* But he couldn't. Ben was right. She had to sleep with the other women.

Jonathan yawned, his eyelids suddenly heavy. He yawned again and rolled on to his side. His eyelids drooped.

Chapter 6

The First Clue

The persistent shaking dragged Ben out of the dream he'd been enjoying. He opened his eyes. Two faces swam into view.

"Come on lazy bones." Jonathan released his hold on Ben's shoulder and straightened up.

"Oh… do go away." Ben rolled on to his other side.

"Lazy bones… what is this lazy bones?" Robert looked puzzled.

Ben stiffened. He turned and looked at Robert, his eyes widening with apprehension. He scrambled to his feet. "Er… forget it. What's for breakfast?"

"Idiot!"

Robert stared as Jonathan pushed Ben towards the door.

Once out of the compound, Robert led the way across to a narrow path on top of the ridge. The sun was only just creeping over the horizon yet already down in the valley a line of workers was moving methodically through waist-high corn. Scythes glistened in the sunlight, the blades swinging backwards and forwards.

"For goodness sake Ben," Jonathan snapped dropping a little behind so Robert wouldn't be able to hear. "What were you thinking?"

"I was confused. I'd forgotten where we were. I'd only just woken up, remember?" Ben glared at him.

"Can I suggest that it would be a good idea if you thought next time before speaking?" said Jonathan quickening his pace again.

Ben glared at his back. "Oh really," he shouted. "You're a fine one to talk. Who was it who introduced 'lazy bones' into the Norman vocabulary? Yes – all right – I agree – I should have remembered breakfast hadn't been invented but I didn't. It was a genuine mistake – okay?"

Jonathan stopped in mid-stride and swung round. "You seemed to make rather a lot of gen…" Catching Ben's eye he broke off his face reddening – he knew he was on shaky ground. Robert *had* noticed his 'lazy bones'. He hunched his shoulders and said more quietly: "Okay, so we both made mistakes. Let's agree to be more careful in the future?"

Ben nodded. "Yeah…good idea. Now we'd better get going again." He frowned. "Hey, that's odd… where's Robert… don't say he's disappeared, too?"

Jonathan spun round and shaded his eyes against the sun. There was no sign of the young Norman. He scowled. Was it happening again?

"No, it's all right. Look… down there," Ben said pointing at a figure climbing out of a dip in the ground.

Jonathan laughed with relief. "Hey, Robert," he yelled. "Hang on… wait for us."

"It's no good, he can't hear," Ben said. "Come on. We'd better run."

Slithering and sliding they skidded down the path, sending streams of pebbles and dirt cascading down the slope in front of them.

When the first ones rolled past Robert he turned and waited, hands on hips. "You must keep up," he said as Jonathan and Ben caught him up. He frowned. "There is much to be done at harvest time. I cannot go out to the men in the fields until I have left you, Jonathan, at the forge and taken you, Ben, to the mill."

"The forge, huh? Of course. I'd forgotten you're going to work in the forge." Ben grinned at Jonathan. "My word, you will get hot… very hot. I'll think of you when I'm having a dip in the river."

Ben was right! It *was* hot in the forge. Unpleasantly hot. Jonathan pumped the bellows furiously sending sparks flying out of the fire. Outside the sun beat incessantly on the thatched roof. Between the two the temperature in the wooden shack soared until it was almost unbearable.

"Eh, lad." Steam filled the hut when Conrad plunged another red-hot ploughshare into the trough of water by his feet. "Didn't yeh hear what I said?"

Jonathan shook his head. He'd stopped listening sometime ago to the blacksmith who'd been rabbiting-on from the moment he'd arrived. By now his head ached and his mouth was dry. He knew if he didn't sit down soon he'd probably fall over.

"I said – you dun well." Conrad raised his voice above the hissing and sizzling. "Better'n I expected. The morning's nearly dun. We'll take a rest." He wiped the sweat streaming down his face with the back of his hairy arm. "Go on outside. Find a place in the shade. I'll join yer shortly."

Jonathan let go of the bellows. Rubbing his cramped fingers he walked slowly towards the door and out into the yard. There was only a bit of shade, under a scraggy apple tree. He lay down in it and closed his eyes.

"Ere, drink this."

Jonathan opened his eyes.

The blacksmith was bending over him, a cracked earthenware jug in his massive hand. He grinned. "T'is good. Straight from t' well. I drew it meself."

Licking his parched lips, Jonathan sat up and reached for the jug.

Snnoorr… sch…sch…sch… snnoorr… sch…sch… sch… snnoorr…

Jonathan shoved his fingers in both ears.

Snnoorr… sch…sch…sch… snnoorr…

He glared at the blacksmith who was lying on his back next to him. He'd never be able to sleep with that noise going on. Should he prod him? No, it probably wouldn't work.

Disgruntled, he got to his feet. There wasn't a lot to see… a few scraggy bushes, the apple tree, the well by the door of the hut. He walked over to the door and leaned against the wooden post of the porch, his mind racing.

Why were they here? What were they meant to do? There had to be a reason. Jonathan kicked a small stone and watched it roll across the ground. He shivered. The trouble was he couldn't think of a reason and that scared him. Because without one how on earth would they find their way back to the twenty-first century?

He glanced up despondently… and blinked. Row upon row of carvings decorated the smoke-stained lintel. Some were little more than primitive scratches, others were simple pictures of everyday life; a few were so intricate, only a skilled craftsman could have carved them into the hard wood.

Despite a growing crick in his neck, he wandered the length of the porch studying each one in turn. Occasionally he would reach up to touch one that particularly appealed to him. It was fascinating how they let him see the different dimensions of life in a medieval community.

"Eh lad, what are you looking at?"

Jonathan jerked around. For a large man the blacksmith moved surprisingly quietly. A moment ago he'd been snoring in the shade of the apple tree – now he was standing behind Jonathan watching him curiously.

Jonathan pointed at the beam. "Those."

"Oh, them." Clearly bored, Conrad took a sickle from the top of the pile of broken tools in the corner of the porch.

"They're good," said Jonathan. "Did you do them?"

"Nay, different folk carved 'em." Conrad tested the cutting edge of the bent blade with a grimy thumb. "People waiting fer their tools. Friends waiting fer me to finish fer the day." He tilted his head and studied them more closely as though seeing them for the first time. "Here…" he tapped a tiny horse and cart. "This were dun by Thomas the carter. A wheel came off the haywain at the beginning of harvest. He carved that while waiting fer it to be mended. Over there…" he broke off hearing a sharp exclamation. "What lad?"

With an uneasy laugh, Jonathan pointed at one in the centre of the beam. "That one… who did it?" he asked feeling for the chain around his neck.

The blacksmith frowned. "I dun rightly know." He scratched his ear. "Looks quite old. Let me think… Yeah, it were probably dun when me father worked the forge."

"How can you tell?"

"S'easy! See, the wood's darkened around these rings. And look 'ow worn this be." Conrad traced the shape of the harp in the middle ring with the tip of his finger.

The chain ran through Jonathan's fingers until they came to the talisman. Grasping it he swallowed. Why was an identical symbol to the one on his star carved on the beam? Except… no he was wrong… it wasn't identical. There was that harp.

"Eh lad," the blacksmith poked him with the handle of the sickle. "Now I remembers. I were naught but a boy when me father showed it me. Young Edgar carved it."

51

His eyes still fixed on the three rings, Jonathan said: "Young Edgar?"

"Aye, the son of the last Saxon Lord. He were a gentle lad. Some days he'd come and sit in one of them corners, ever so quiet like and watch me father work the forge. Sometimes he'd pump the fire – like you bin; other times he'd take out a stick and do a bit of whittling. But you should talk to the musician about him."

"The musician?"

"Aye! He used ter visit the village when Edgar was but a lad. It were 'im that taught him 'ow to play his harp."

"His harp?" Jonathan sagged, suddenly deflated. So that was why it was in the carving. Except... he tried to shrug off his gloom... it didn't explain those interlocking rings.

"Aye, lad!" Conrad was beginning to sound a little bit irritated by the constant repetitions. "A harp – like the one – up there." He pointed.

"Did you say he left here when the Normans came?"

Conrad shook his head. "Nay, his parents and sisters left the village." He cleared his throat. "Young Edgar's still here."

Jonathan's eyes lit up. This was more like it. He'd find this Edgar and talk to him. Perhaps they'd learn something from him.

But his hopes were dashed when the blacksmith added sombrely "...aye... the lad lies with his ancestors – in the churchyard."

"Oh!"

"The poor boy took sick and died. Happened not long after he'd finished that very carving if I remembers right. Near broke his mother's heart." With that Conrad tossed the sickle back on the pile. "Right. Fetch in some wood. 'Tis time we got that fire going again."

Chapter 7
The Message

"Victoria!"

Very carefully Victoria folded the delicate shawl and placed it in the trunk before peering around the screen shielding her from the rest of the occupants of the antechamber.

"Victoria," the petulant voice repeated. "Where are you?"

"Here m'lady." She stepped out into the open.

"Huh! And what pray are you doing?'

"Packing your linen m'lady, ready for when you leave – for your new home."

"Well stop doing that. I want you to brush my hair." Adela's voice was growing shriller.

Victoria sighed. Only a few more items and another chest could have been strapped up, ready to go. She closed the lid, brushed the worst of the dust from her skirt then walked slowly over to where Adela was waiting.

As she approached, a servant girl handed her a tortoiseshell hairbrush. Victoria smiled at her, stepped up behind her mistress and began brushing the long brown tresses with swift even strokes. Adela held up a silver hand-mirror and examined her reflection in the glass, all the time primping and preening.

Victoria frowned and looked over her mistress's shoulder. All she could see in the glass was a swirling dense mist. When it started to break up she could see the shape of a face. But it wasn't the face she'd expected to see. She twisted the brush nervously. "Sylvene?"

"Ahh…" The mirror slipped to the floor. Adela's hands flew to her head. "What do you think you're doing?" she shrieked.

"Oh… m'lady!" Her hands trembling, Victoria wrenched at the tangled hair caught in the bristles.

"Stop it," Adela screamed. "Stop it at once… you're hurting."

"I'm sorry, m'lady." Victoria took a deep breath then another. After the third she felt herself beginning to steady. Very carefully she started unwinding the hair from the bristles.

Adela flinched when the even strokes began again. "Be more careful this time," she snapped. She stamped her foot and pointed. The nearest maid rushed forward, picked up the mirror, curtseyed and handed it to the young woman.

Again Sylvene, her face pale and drawn, her eyes dark with anxiety, gazed at Victoria, this time with a finger to her lips. Seeing the question in Victoria's eyes she shook her head and vanished.

Victoria's hand trembled. Had Sylvene's appearance simply been her imagination running riot? No, definitely

not! That *had* been her face in the mirror – not Adela's…
but what did it mean? What was happening? Her mind
racing, she handed the brush to the maid and began
plaiting Adela's hair.

But behind her cool exterior her mind continued to
whirl. Somehow she had to get hold of the mirror. Could
she do it now without anyone noticing? The trouble was
she didn't have any pockets and with her luck if she
tucked it under her apron it would probably fall out and
shatter.

Could she come back after the evening meal? It
shouldn't be too difficult to slip away. As long as the
mirror was back by the morning no one would need to
know… except… there was always a slight possibility
Adela might want it before going to bed. Victoria shrugged
and fastened the plait with a ribbon. That was a risk she'd
have to take. She started braiding the second plait.

She was just finishing when the door flew open and a
young man entered the room. He made his way to Adela
and bowed.

"What is it?"

"M'lord bids you join him in the stables."

A faint smile flickered across Adela's face. She
clapped her hands. "Be quick, Victoria," she said tapping
her foot impatiently. Victoria tied the second plait and
covered her head with the wimple. Then she placed the
flowing couvre-chef on top and stepped back. Adela
beckoned to the two maids whispering to each other.
"Matilda, Mary, attend to me." She thrust the mirror at

Victoria. "You… stay and tidy up." With a toss of her head, she walked from the room, the two girls chattering excitedly behind her.

The door closed. Victoria stared at the mirror. Once again an opaque grey mist covered the glass. Her heart racing she waited, watching the mist disperse very slowly. When the glass was clear Sylvene's face reappeared. "Victoria, you have to find the Sun..." she said quietly.

"Find the sun? What do you mean? Why do we have to find the sun? Tell me Sylvene. We need to know why we're here."

"I'm trying to explain… and I don't have much time. Now listen carefully. You must find the Sun before a man called the *Gleeman*…"

"The Gleeman!"

"Do stop interrupting." Sylvene's voice was tense. "Listen, someone called the Gleeman also seeks the Sun. If he finds it everything will be lost. Do you understand? He must not find it. Without it none of you will be able to return home."

The colour drained from Victoria's face as the glass was once again covered in a swirling mist. Clutching the mirror she slumped against the wall.

It seemed like forever but eventually the blacksmith threw down his hammer and straightened up with a groan. "You c'n go lad." He arched his back. "Ah, that's better. Yeah, work's dun fer the day." He undid his leather apron and grabbed a ladle from a hook on the wall which he filled with water from the bucket by his feet and drained at a gulp.

"Ah… that's good." Conrad grinned at Jonathan. "Yep… better get going lad, before I changes me mind." He lifted the bucket and tipped the rest of the water over his head. "Go on. Just make sure you'm here by sunrise."

"Don't you want me to help tidy up?"

Conrad shook his head and drops of water flew out of his hair. "Nah… there's little enough to do," he said.

By the time Jonathan reached the path to the compound the sun was dipping towards the horizon – a large golden ball its fiery flashes spreading across the sky. But he didn't notice. He was too busy thinking about the carving; the rings; Edgar; the harp. What worried him was whether or not Ben and Victoria would be able to understand their importance. It might be difficult convincing them of the significance of the three rings, he knew. But surely once he showed them his pendant they'd have an idea of what he was trying to say…

A welcome breeze sprang up. He stopped, enjoying the cool air brushing against his face. It had been hot in the forge – oppressively hot. If he were at home, he'd be heading for the shower right now...

The thought stabbed him like a physical pain. He staggered. Much better *not* to think about home. He fixed his mind on the others. Victoria… she was more sensible than Ben. He'd find her first and tell her everything. The thought of home receded a little. He set off again.

He'd been walking for some time when the slow, harsh cry of the seagulls circling overhead finally penetrated his thoughts. The hairs on the back of his neck stood up and he shivered as a gull flew past, its yellow unblinking eye fixed on his face. He felt for his talisman suddenly filled with doubts. Should he show it to the others? He'd never shown it to anyone before.

"Jonathan!"

He spun round and was shocked to see Robert was watching him from further up the hillside.

"Robert!"

Robert smiled. "You were deep in thought. Will you come with me? There is something I would like you to see."

"Er… can't it wait?" asked Jonathan. "I was hoping to find Victoria."

Robert shook his head. He smiled wryly. "That is not a good idea. My sister will not thank you if you interrupt one of her maids while she is working."

Maids!

Jonathan choked. Although he hadn't known Victoria for very long he was pretty certain she wouldn't appreciate being called a 'maid' by anyone. "In that case," he said evenly. "I'll go and find Ben."

"Hmm… do you want your brother to get into more trouble?"

Jonathan shook his head.

"I thought not. The miller is a hard man which is why the Bailiff wanted Ben to work there. My advice is come with me. You can talk to your brother and sister at the evening meal."

Without waiting to see if he took his advice Robert set off up the hill, his cloak swinging from side to side with each lengthening stride. Jonathan hesitated then sighed. Oh, well, Robert was right – what he had to tell them could wait until the evening.

They walked swiftly past the compound and on towards the top of the ridge. Far, far below a silver ribbon of water snaked along the bottom of the valley. In a field alongside the river row upon golden row of stooks waited for the ramshackled cart heading their way. In the distance a line of reapers was moving through more shimmering corn, their scythes slicing through the stalks.

Jonathan glanced at a rocky outcrop on the side of the hill. He flinched as Robert jumped on to it and made a sweeping circle with his hand. "This is what I wanted to show you," the young Norman called, his voice bleak.

Holding his breath Jonathan waited nervously while the slim, straight figure stared across the valley, his cloak fluttering in the breeze. "I wish you'd come down," he said at last.

"Yes," Robert said, paying no attention. "One day all this will be mine."

"Really I don't think you should stand…"

"Stop worrying, Jonathan and listen. I do not want this. I would prefer to take Holy Orders. But King

William gave my grandfather this village and all the land as far as we can see – for his valour on the battlefield at Hastings. It is natural for my father to want it to remain in the family. I am the only son," he shrugged, "so a marriage has been arranged…"

"An arranged marriage!"

"A son must obey his father," Robert said, his eyes empty.

"Where I come from people choose their own…" Jonathan bit his lip suddenly aware of Robert's puzzled glance.

"Choose their own what?"

"Er… um…" stuttered Jonathan trying frantically to think of a way out of the tight spot he'd got himself into. "What I meant to say was that my father…"

"…your father…?"

For a minute Jonathan couldn't think why Robert still sounded surprised – then he realised… and quickly covered his second mistake. "Er… yes… before he died, my father told me I should do what I thought would be right for me."

"Ah… I envy you. If my family had not been given the land there would be no conflict – but the land is important to them."

"What about the Saxons?"

"The Saxons?"

"Yes, the people who lived here before your family came." Jonathan was surprised how normal his voice sounded. "Where did they go?"

"I do not know. They were Saxons. They must have left when news that their King had been defeated reached the village. Only the peasants were here when my grandfather arrived." He held up a hand. "Listen. What do you hear?"

Straining his ears Jonathan heard the distant chimes. "The meal bell!"

Robert leapt on to the path. "I thought so. We should go now."

Chapter 8

A Moon and Two Stars

"We need to talk," Victoria said urgently, leaning over the table.

The evening meal was over; the musician was playing his flute. For the second night in a row the trestle table had been pushed against the back wall.

"What about?" asked Ben curiously.

Victoria glanced around the room. Apart from those sitting at the High Table everyone else was either huddled into small groups or sitting on the benches lining the walls waiting for something to happen. A low hum filled the air. "Not here," she said in a tight voice. "Too many people. Let's go outside."

"Outside?" grumbled Ben. "Why? I'm tired. Have either of you any idea what it's like carrying huge sacks of corn around on your back all day long? Can't we just sit here and do nothing?"

"No," Jonathan said bluntly. "I've got some news, too. Come on."

Dusk was beginning to fall. Jonathan stood in the doorway searching for somewhere quiet; somewhere where they wouldn't be noticed when the rest of the villagers returned to the sleeping quarters for the night.

He glanced to the right and saw a narrow gap between the hall and the women's sleeping quarters just wide enough for a person. "This way," he whispered and led them into it. Once or twice they had to turn sideways and squeeze through a tighter space. But eventually they reached the fence.

Jonathan glanced back up the passage. "We should be safe enough here... *Ben*..." his voice shook with anger. "What do you think you're doing?"

"Trying to find somewhere to sit," said Ben scrambling on top of the kitchen woodpile stacked against the back of the Hall.

Jonathan closed his eyes. "I don't believe it... will you never learn? The whole lot will come down if you're not careful..."

"Oh stop fussing. I can look after myself. Just get on with whatever it is you want to tell us... I want to go to bed."

Jonathan glared at him. "All right; but first I'd like to hear what Victoria's got to say."

Ben threw down a couple of logs and grinned when one rolled over Jonathan's foot. Settling himself in the hollow he'd made he chucked a twig at Victoria. "Well... tell us."

"Don't do that." She turned her back on him. "It was something that happened when I was brushing Adela's hair earlier this afternoon," she said to Jonathan. "She was looking in a mirror and I saw..." Victoria bit her lip.

"Your own reflection? So what? Did you break the glass?" Ben was the only one to laugh at the feeble joke.

The other two stared at him, exasperated.

"No I didn't," snapped Victoria. "Anyway it wasn't my face… it was Sylvene's…in the glass."

"Oh yeah!" Ben sniggered. "And what did she do – blow you a kiss?"

"No," shouted Victoria almost crying with rage. "She gave me a message."

"Ooh, a mes…"

"Shut up Ben. Carry on Victoria."

Victoria shot Jonathan a grateful look. "It was quite simple. She said we had to search for the Sun."

"Why? It is night time after all. Don't worry. It'll be back in the morning, unless it's raining of course."

"Now you're being ridiculous, Ben," Jonathan said shortly. "*Search for the Sun…* Victoria, have you any idea what she meant?"

"Perhaps there's going to be an eclipse," Ben suggested.

Victoria cast him a withering look. "I don't think so. There was more. She said we had to be very careful because there's someone else looking for the Sun. Someone called the Gleeman. She said that if he found it first we'd never get home… Oh Jonathan," she wailed, "I don't want to be stuck here forever."

"'Gleeman'… I've heard that name before." Jonathan frowned and then shrugged his shoulders. "What do you think she meant by – *Search for the Sun*?"

"I wish she'd told Victoria how we could get home," said Ben with feeling.

"Don't you ever listen? According to Sylvene if we don't find this Sun we'll probably end up stuck here for ever."

"Yes, and do you know something else – Jonathan was right – if you keep on wriggling around like that, the whole lot'll come down," Victoria said priggishly. She moved out of the way as a log rolled off the top of the pile and landed with a thud against the fence.

Ben wasn't listening. Kneeling precariously he was peering into the lengthening shadows. "Who's there?" he said sharply. "Come on out. I know you're in there – I heard you."

Jonathan glanced at him angrily then frowned. It was obvious from Ben's expression that he wasn't fooling this time. "Stay here while I take a look," he said moving forward.

As he spoke a tall figure stepped from the shadows and bowed. It was the musician. "My apologies friends, I did not mean to startle you."

They stared at him suspiciously.

"You are strangers here I believe, like myself," he continued.

"Are you a stranger?" said Jonathan. "I was told that you'd been here before."

"Once or twice," the man said smoothly. "My travels take me far and wide."

"What were you doing just now – listening to us?"

The musician shook his head. "I wanted to find somewhere to sleep. It was too hot in the hall last night.

I thought it might be cooler out here. Where are you going – when you leave the village?"

Jonathan frowned, taken by surprise at the sudden change of subject. He eyed the musician, warily. "London sir… we hope to find work there for the winter."

The musician chuckled. "If that is truly your desire, I am sure you will succeed." He glanced at Victoria. "What is your name, child?"

"Victoria, sir"

"Hmm… Victoria. An unusual name – but a pleasing one. And the names of your companions?"

"My brothers, sir," she said with dignity. "My brothers are called Jonathan and Ben. Why do you ask?"

The musician raised an eyebrow. "Mere curiosity child, mere curiosity. When do you plan to leave?"

"Not until the harvest is safely in. We told Sir Henry we would help with it," said Ben bringing more logs down as he jumped off the woodpile. "You ask an awful lot of questions. Why are you so interested in us?"

"That is all it is – just interest. Ah well, no doubt we will meet again." Humming softly the man sauntered away and disappeared into the darkness again.

Victoria grabbed Jonathan's arm. "Do you think he heard what we were saying?"

"I don't think so." But Jonathan sounded doubtful. He shook his head.

Victoria's grip tightened around his arm. "What is it?" she demanded.

"I don't know; there's something about that man…

something I can't explain."

"For heaven's sakes, how much longer do we have to stay out here? Jonathan if you want to tell us something please get a move on. I really do need to go to bed."

"Of course… sorry… It might sound a bit of an anti-climax after Victoria's news but I think it could be important. I found a carving at the forge."

"A carving – oh very exciting," Ben said sneeringly. "Right, I'm off."

"No wait – there is more. It was a carving of a harp… on the beam of the porch. I know what you're thinking but before you go have a look at this." Jonathan undid the clasp of the chain around his neck and held up a tiny gold star.

Ben and Victoria stared, wide-eyed as he turned the star over and pointed at an engraving on the back. "What caught my attention was that the harp was in the centre of three rings… like these." He glanced up suddenly aware of the growing tension. "What?" he said sharply.

A muscle twitched at the side of Ben's mouth. Silently he pulled a chain from under his tunic. A moment later he too held up a star… identical to the one Jonathan was holding.

Jonathan drew in his breath. "I can see what you're thinking," he said, at last. "But mine's got…" Without saying a word, Ben turned his star over. Jonathan's voice trailed away.

"Here… move out of the way." Victoria edged past him and grabbed Ben's star. Her eyes widened.

"Well?"

She stood quite still her breath coming in tiny gasps. "It's nothing Jonathan … no what am I saying… it's not nothing… it's…"

"It's what?"

"Those rings!"

"What about them?" said Ben retrieving his star and fastening the chain around his neck.

Victoria stared at the ground for what seemed like ages. When she looked up her expression was deadly serious. "I've seen those rings before."

"Really? Where?" Jonathan sounded startled.

"On the back of a moon."

Ben snorted. "Au – come on – the back of a moon! What moon?"

Jonathan shot Victoria a strange searching look. "Show me." He held out his hand.

"How did you know?" she asked removing the couvre-chef from her head.

"Your face," said Jonathan, "gives you away every time. Take it from me – you'd be no good at poker."

Victoria blushed a little and pushed back her wimple. Now Jonathan could see the chain.

"Shall I?" he asked.

She nodded and tilted her head forward.

"Poker!" said Ben, confused. "Why would she want to play poker?"

"She doesn't – here, look at this." Jonathan handed him the gold moon.

Ben let out a long, low whistle. "I don't believe it.

Three sets of rings… and three talismans."

"Four sets of rings. Don't forget I saw one at the forge."

Ben nodded. "And you're saying they look like these?"

"I am – exactly the same… except…"

"Except what? Here Victoria, you'd better put it away." Ben thrust the moon into her hands.

"I told you – there was a harp carved in the middle."

"What do you think that means?" said Victoria, puzzled.

"I wish I knew," Jonathan said. "But the blacksmith told me who carved it."

A door slammed. "It must be bedtime," whispered Ben, hearing voices.

"Quick Jonathan," said Victoria.

"It was carved by a Saxon boy, called Edgar. According to Conrad – he's the blacksmith – this Edgar was the son of the last Saxon Lord of the Manor."

"Oh!" Ben sounded disappointed. "Then he must have done it ages ago, probably long before the Normans came. I can't see how that helps."

Jonathan shrugged. "Neither can I. But there was something else. Conrad told me Edgar died before the conquest. He's buried in the churchyard."

"Dead!" exclaimed Victoria. She slumped to the ground and covered her face with her hands.

"Don't," said Jonathan stooping a little to put a tentative arm on her shoulder. "Please don't."

Victoria glanced up. "It's all very well saying 'don't,'" she said crossly. "But if he's dead how on earth can we find out why he put a harp in the rings?"

"Listen," said Jonathan, determined to remain positive. "The fact that we've found these rings is, I think, important. It can't just be a co-incidence. They're much too much alike. It could mean we've been brought here for a reason. Don't you see, I think we were meant to find that carving? It's obviously some kind of clue. Perhaps we need to find the harp."

"Possibly, but aren't you forgetting something… when the Saxons left wouldn't they have taken all their things?" said Ben.

Jonathan shook his head. "I don't think so. I think they'd have left empty handed. Their King was dead. There was a new one on the throne. Soldiers were everywhere hunting them down. No, I think they would have left in too much of a hurry to worry about a harp." Jonathan crossed his fingers behind his back, hopefully.

"In that case…" said Victoria.

"Victoria!"

She stiffened. "Someone's calling me. I'd better go. We'll talk again tomorrow." Gathering up her skirts she disappeared into the darkness.

Chapter 9
Wedding Preparations

Motes of dust swirled through the shaft of sunlight streaming into the barn. Ben stared at the earthen floor disconsolately. How much longer would he have to go on shovelling corn into sacks? They'd been doing it since dawn. Every muscle ached. His nose and eyes were clogged with dust.

He glanced at his hands and shuddered. They were covered in raw and weeping blisters. Propping the spade against the nearest wall he shuffled, like an old man, to the door and leaned against the frame enjoying the warmth of the sun which was beginning to set. He gulped down mouthfuls of fresh air. They must have been working for hours. He grinned momentarily pleased he'd learned how to tell the time by the sun.

But the grin vanished as quickly as it had come. Okay – so he could do that but he was no closer to finding the harp and that's what he really wanted to do. He needed to prove to the others he wasn't as stupid as they thought.

"I know…"

"Know what, boy?"

Ben blinked. He hadn't realised he'd spoken out-loud. He turned. One of the men from the working party was leaning on his spade, watching him curiously. He smiled cautiously at the weather-beaten face. "Er… nothing really... it's just that I need to go outside for a few minutes," he said with an embarrassed laugh.

The man smirked. "Then you'd better go, boy. Mind yer be quick. If the Bailiff comes and sees yer not working, well… yer knows what to expect." He raised his eyebrows.

Ben swallowed. He certainly did know what to expect. "Don't worry, I won't be long," he said hurriedly.

Out in the open he hesitated. The question was… where to look? Stamping hooves caught his attention. He looked across the yard at the open stable door. Why not try in there?

He took a step then stopped. It was too risky. People were going in and out of that building all the time. He should choose somewhere closer – perhaps the barn to his left. He glanced around again. There was no one about. He ran to the barn, pushed the door and peered inside. It was full of corn. Ben kicked angrily at the ground sending a shower of dust into the air.

Grimacing he backed away. Did it have to be the stables after all? His eyes fell on a much smaller building tucked into a corner behind the stables and half-hidden by an overgrown bush.

Strange, he thought. Why hadn't he noticed it before?

A shout of laughter broke the silence. Ben jumped. He looked around but the compound was still empty. It must have come from the barn where he'd been working he decided.

Well, he'd better get on with it. Taking a deep breath he ran, crouching a little and keeping well into the shadows of the fence. Approaching the barn he stared. The roof must once have been covered in thatch but there was only a tiny section left. Even that was beginning to sag under the moss.

The window was boarded up. The door tilted at a crazy angle, hanging from a single hinge. Ben pushed it gently then froze. Something was moving – away to his right.

He turned very slowly. A man was standing in the stable doorway. Ben shivered. He didn't need to see the face. He'd recognise the squat figure of the Bailiff anywhere.

He felt sick. There was no escape. It could only be a matter of time before he was seen. And when he was... he swayed and clutched the crumbling doorframe. Steadying himself he waited his eyes fixed on the whip in the Bailiff's hands.

There was a shout from inside the stable. At once the Bailiff turned and disappeared back inside. Ben let out a long juddering sigh. His heart thumping he slipped into the barn and – stared. It was stacked to the roof with broken furniture and discarded tools.

Very slowly he walked over to a table and ran his hand along a huge scar that had been gouged into the top. He smiled. Surely Edgar would have thought this barn was the perfect hiding place for his harp?

Trembling with excitement, Ben knelt in the dust and began rummaging through the contents of a basket.

The sound of thudding hooves echoed along the valley as a small group of riders emerged from the forest. One by one the men in the field lowered their scythes; behind them the women building the rows of stooks also stopped to watch the galloping horses thunder by.

"Bah!" A workman recognised the leading rider with his purple cloak streaming out behind. "'Tis the King." He spat noisily into the palm of his hands. Turning his back on the horsemen he began cutting the corn again.

Sir Henry strode purposefully across the compound. Behind him Robert and the Bailiff hurried to keep up. They waited in the gateway and watched the line of horses galloping up the hill, manes and tails flying on the wind. Sir Henry turned to the Bailiff. "Go – make sure everything is as it should be before the King arrives."

The Bailiff frowned, disappointment written across his face. But he knew his master. Muttering under his breath he bowed and backed away. However the disappointment quickly vanished when, hearing a noise, he stopped by the ramshackled barn and went inside.

"Well, well, well," he said, rubbing his hands with glee. "What have we here?"

Startled, Ben spun round.

"Where is that girl?" Adela tapped her foot impatiently early the following morning.

"Girl, madam?"

"Yes fool. Victoria! I want her to dress me – not you with your rough hands. You can go and help in the fields."

Her eyes lowered the maid curtseyed and backed away. But once Adela had turned to speak to another woman she spun on her heel and stormed over to the nearest door. The way led her past Victoria, who was kneeling in front of an open chest clutching a shawl and staring into space.

The maid tapped her shoulder. "*She* wants you," she said, eyes flashing.

Victoria looked back at Adela then up at the maid.

"Yes, *her*. And you're welcome. She's in a right mood."

Victoria sighed. There was so much to think about. That was one reason why she was trying to keep out of the bride's way. Unfortunately, despite all her thinking, she was no further forward to finding an answer. For a start there were all those rings. She hadn't liked to admit it to either of the boys but she didn't completely understand the significance of those.

Then there were the quarrels. There'd been another last night. A stupid quarrel; one that had started because of Ben's warped sense of humour. He'd seemed to think it was funny that the Bailiff had caught him searching the barn. Jonathan hadn't. "*So… now he's got another reason to be suspicious about us*," he'd raged when Ben had told them what had happened.

Ben had fuelled Jonathan's anger by shrugging and saying: "*So what?*" And then he'd made things even worse by describing how he'd been dragged off by the Bailiff to see Sir Henry – who was talking to the King.

The King... that was something else. They'd been standing by his monument when they'd slipped through time – a monument describing his death. Yet now they were here and he was still alive. Not only was he still alive he was actually in the next room!

"*Victoria!*"

The shrill voice dragged her away from her thoughts. Putting the shawl into the chest she stood up and reluctantly walked to where the bride was waiting.

"Dress me." Adela pointed at a chemise hanging over the back of a chair.

Biting back a retort, Victoria curtseyed and picked up the linen petticoat. She slipped it over the bride's head and eased it past her shoulders. It tumbled to the ground. She looked round. "The dress," she said softly to a watching maid.

Soon all that could be seen of the bride's feet were a pair of silver slippers peeping out from under the hem of the blue silk wedding gown.

Victoria fastened the girdle around Adela's tiny waist and stepped back.

"Oh," gasped one of the women, "my lady..."

"What?"

"You l...look s...so beautiful," the girl stuttered.

Adela stared at her blankly, then turned to Victoria. "Where is my cloak?"

"Here, madam." The bride's old nurse hobbled forward, the cloak draped across her arms.

"Place it on my shoulders. Careful – mind my wimple! Now fasten it. Quickly... *no*... not like that! Fasten it with the brooch."

"Brooch, m...mistress?"

Adela began tapping her foot again. "Yes, my brooch! The one my Father gave me."

The nurse edged away. She licked her dry lips. "I am afraid I do not know where it is mistress," she whispered.

"Look for it," screeched the bride. "*All* of you – stop what you're doing and look for my brooch. I want it. Today is my wedding day. I want to wear that brooch. *Find it!*"

Frightened, the women scurried round and round... searching... searching... yet never finding. Victoria pursed her lips and leaned against a wall, watching. They'd be lucky to find anything in this chaos she thought – especially something as small as a brooch.

The foot tapping became more frantic. Victoria glanced to her right. Two maids had tipped up a chest and were scrabbling through the contents. She frowned. Things were getting out of hand. If it carried on like this everything would have to be repacked and the bride and groom were leaving in the morning. Well, it could wait until then. *She'd* done enough packing for one day.

She picked her way through mounds of linen scattered across the floor and went up to one of the windows. Half-heartedly she reached up and ran her hand along the top of a shelf just above the frame.

Dust flew into the air then floated down again, settling on her clothes, in her hair, even up her nose. Eyes streaming and sneezing incessantly Victoria mopped her face with her apron then blew her nose. The sneezing stopped. She looked around again... and this time froze.

The recess.... she'd first noticed it a couple of days earlier. Admittedly it didn't look very big. But it was worth a look. Someone might have hidden the brooch in there.

She shivered, aware if that was the case then one of the maids must be a thief.

She glanced around the room. Everywhere was in complete chaos. The maids were crawling around the floor, frantically searching. Adela was still tapping her foot. If she didn't want to be noticed she'd better do something quick.

Victoria skirted the room, taking care not to disturb anyone. Reaching the tiny alcove she examined the opening carefully. A strange half-light flickered just inside the entrance, almost like curtains blowing in a wind. Her throat constricted. She didn't understand why, but she suddenly felt uneasy.

Licking her dry lips she took several deep, even breaths until the panic threatening to overwhelm her began to subside. As her courage returned she crouched in front of the opening. Taking another deep breath she pushed her arm through that half-light.

Behind it was space... nothing but space. She felt

around, desperately. The recess was in fact a cavity, deeper and higher than anything she'd expected. Her hand hit the side of the wall. She winced. Muttering softly she pulled it out and rubbed her knuckles. Then she plunged her arm back into the opening.

This time she felt around the floor. There was nothing there… no wait… her heart leapt as her fingers brushed against something solid – something wedged into a corner.

"My brooch… ah… my brooch."

Victoria whirled around and the object slipped from her grasp. She straightened up and pulled off the mangled cobwebs clinging to her sleeve. On the other side of the room the maids abandoned their search and flocked around Adela, jabbering excitedly.

Victoria reached into the cavity once more and pulled. A trickle of dust and grit poured through the opening, down the side of the wall and over her sandals.

One more tug… She staggered and slid to the floor clutching a battered leather bag. Making sure no one was watching she slowly loosened the knot fastening the neck of the bag.

"Daughter!"

Victoria dropped her apron over the bag and looked up.

Adela swept a deep curtsey. "Papa?"

Sir Henry shook his head and came further into the room. "Mon dieu," he breathed. "Beautiful… quite beautiful." He held out his hand. "Child… we must leave for the church. Your King and your husband awaits."

A shy smile replaced the bride's normal spoilt and petulant look. With her head held high, she placed her hand on her father's arm and let him lead her from the room.

The door closed.

Victoria lifted her apron and stared at the bag lying in her lap. A shiver ran down her spine. She rolled back its neck and peeped inside, then, very carefully lifted out a tiny harp. She held it up. Was this Edgar's missing harp? Shaking a little she stood and with trembling hands pulled away the canvas covering the window.

Sunlight streamed into the room. Victoria poured over the little harp, but it was no good. Wherever she looked there was nothing… nothing that remotely resembled the three rings.

If only, she thought running her fingers across the fraying strings, if only this had been Edgar's harp, things might have turned out all right.

A long sweet note filled the room.

Chapter 10
The Wedding

Victoria sucked the angry weal on her little finger where the string had skimmed away a layer of skin as it broke free. The pain was piercing. Shaking, she fought off a sudden feeling of queasiness, at the same time picking absent-mindedly at the peg at the bottom of the frame. It began to wobble. She wiggled it backwards and forwards. It came away and she placed it on the windowsill before removing some of the frayed pieces of string dangling from the harp.

That was when she noticed the scratches around the hole. Curious, she turned the harp upside down and held it to the light. A grin spread across her face. They weren't scratch marks. They were three perfect rings. Wide-eyed, she traced the shape carved in the middle ring.

"What are you doing?"

Victoria dropped the harp on the windowsill and spun round. A maid was standing in the doorway watching her inquisitively. "Er... nothing!"

"My lady is asking for you," the woman said slowly, her gaze darting from Victoria to the windowsill.

"Tell her I'm coming."

The maid took a step closer. "What were you holding?"

Victoria shook her head. "Nothing!" she repeated. "I've... I'm trying to tidy up, that's all. Tell my lady I am coming."

The maid sniffed and went out of the room. Victoria waited until the door closed then snatched up the leather bag and slipped the harp inside. Fastening the cord around its neck she pushed it back into its hiding place and left the room.

As the door closed behind her the one to the kitchens opened and the musician entered the antechamber. He stopped in front of the recess, a faint smile softening his craggy face.

"So – was there a clue?" Ben demanded.

They were standing slightly apart from the crowd that had gathered around the church gate waiting for the bridal party to reappear.

Victoria glanced at the faces. No one was listening. "Yes – an acorn," she whispered.

Ben spluttered. "An acorn! You're saying we've got to find *one* particular acorn?"

"No! I'm telling you what I saw. It was an acorn."

Jonathan frowned. "Do keep your voice down. People are looking."

"Who cares? I'm fed up with him and his stupid comments. Why does he have to be so... so pigheaded?" Victoria turned away.

Ben snorted, his expression scornful.

Jonathan grabbed her arm. "Wait. Don't go."

"What's the point?" she snapped. "I thought you'd be pleased when I told you about the harp... not... not... so critical. How stupid can you be?"

"We're not... I mean we are pleased. Victoria, stay. We'll talk about it later – when we're alone – I promise."

Victoria swallowed. "Oh, all right, but it's only because I don't want to make a fuss." She glared fiercely at Ben.

The door of the church opened and an air of anticipation rippled through the crowd. The priest led the procession into the sunlight and stepped to one side to let the King pass.

His red hair glinting in the sunshine, the King marched down the path to where a chestnut horse was waiting by the gate. Jonathan watched enviously as he threw back his cloak, took the reins from the groom and put his foot in a stirrup. Holding on to the pummel he swung himself into the saddle.

The horse snorted, stamped at the cobblestones and reared.

Somebody screamed.

Flailing hooves pawed the air.

Settling himself deeper into the saddle the King threw back his head and laughed. He leaned forward until he was almost lying on the horse's neck. Its centre of gravity altered, the animal landed on all fours with a thud.

Outwardly calm the King gathered up the reins; flicked his whip over the horse's rump and drove his spurs into its flanks. Eyes rolling wildly and with specks of foam flying from its mouth the chestnut plunged forward, scattering the people as it set off at a gallop.

Everyone turned to watch until horse and rider had disappeared. From behind a clump of trees, three more horsemen appeared and poured down the hill in hot pursuit.

Jonathan nudged Victoria. "Look!"

Standing in the doorway of the church, were the bride and groom. A great cheer erupted from the watching villagers. Smiling happily Adela and her husband – followed by the rest of the bridal party – walked down the path in a more seemly fashion than their royal master had done, pausing occasionally to talk to a member of the crowd.

Even so Victoria did not expect Adela to notice her.

She did.

Clutching her husband's arm the young woman stopped and nodded. "Merci Victoria."

For once speechless, Victoria watched them go.

"I thought you said…" Ben whispered in her ear.

"I did… and she was." Victoria changed the subject. "Have either of you noticed – we're almost the only people left?"

"The feast!"

Victoria and Jonathan stared at Ben.

He wriggled self-consciously. "One of the men I was working with yesterday said there'd be a special feast today to celebrate the wedding."

"A special feast – what are we waiting for?" demanded Jonathan. "I don't know about you two – but I'm starving."

Linking arms they ran down the hill, the sun warm on their faces. Jonathan caught Ben's eye and smiled. Ben grinned back and started to say something. But his words were drowned by childish shouts and laughter. They stopped and watched the stream of children rushing up the path towards them.

"My apologies," said a soft voice.

The musician was standing behind them.

"There's no need to apologize," said Jonathan quickly.

"You are generous young master – but indeed there is. I am responsible for the young folk's unseemly haste. I have been teaching them a new dance. Now they are anxious to perform it in front of their King."

"Are they? Well I hope they wait 'til we get to the Hall. I would like to see it," said Jonathan.

The musician beamed. "It is kind of you to say so, young master. May I wish you and your companions peace in your time on this special day?"

Despite the sun, Jonathan shivered.

A small and very grubby hand crept around the musician and tugged at his cloak.

"Why have you stopped?" a soft voice murmured.

The musician laughed and swept the child into his arms.

Recognising the blacksmith's daughter Jonathan relaxed a little.

Chuckling, the little girl reached up and touched the man's nose with the tip of her finger. "Please Gleeman hurry – I want to dance."

A tense silence fell over the small group. A wry smile crept over the musician's face. Placing the child on his shoulders he continued up the hill playing a defiant tune on his flute.

"Who's that?" whispered Victoria to the woman sitting on her left.

"Henry, the miller – the miserable sod."

"Oh!" Victoria glanced at him curiously.

"Why does he keep looking at you?" said Jonathan turning to Ben, puzzled.

He shrugged. "How should I know?"

"You must know… you work for him."

"There's no need to remind me," snapped Ben. "I was quite enjoying myself 'til you started talking about him. If you must know we had a bit of a row yesterday."

Jonathan frowned. The miller was still staring at Ben, an unpleasant sneer on his face. What was it like, he wondered, working for someone like him? He eyed the burly figure uncertainly then looked a few places further along the table where Conrad was sitting, talking and laughing with his neighbours. How lucky he was. Before he could say anything to Ben the door behind the High Table opened and a long line of servants trooped in, each carrying a steaming, laden tray.

The room quickly filled with a mixture of mouth-watering smells. Jonathan sniffed appreciatively.

There were trays of whole salmons; haunches of venison; suckling pigs and stuffed pheasants – some had even been re-dressed in their natural plumage when they came out of the ovens. There were peas, onions and beans; cheeses – some soft some hard; herbal salads, bowls of nuts and fruits; reed baskets over-flowing with newly baked bread.

The leading servants peeled away from the line and approached the High Table. Bowing, they knelt before the King and held up their trays for him to choose. The rest of the servants walked into the centre of the Hall and fanned out into two rows. Each taking one side of the table they covered the trenchers with hot, steaming food.

Six more servants entered. Two made for the dais to pour Sir Henry's precious French wine into the golden goblets set out on the crisp linen tablecloth. The rest went straight to the lower table and began distributing jugs of home-brewed ale.

"Music!"

Silence fell over the Hall. Still chewing the guests turned to look at the High Table.

"Music – I say!"

The King leapt to his feet and thumped the table.

Everyone watched warily. A man, a few seats along from Victoria, got up. A second followed almost immediately. A faint buzz filled the Hall as the men made their way to where the Gleeman was waiting by the fire.

As they approached, he raised his flute to his lips and began playing a catchy tune.

Kneeling beside a bag that had been left by the back wall one of the men took out a harp, similar to the one Victoria had found earlier that day. As he drew his fingers across the strings his companion began polishing the mouthpiece of a horn. Soon a burst of music flooded the room.

The King turned to his left and bowed. He held out his hand. Blushing faintly Adela rose and took his arm. For a few moments they danced alone in the centre of the Hall, then – one by one – they were joined on the floor by half a dozen other couples.

Chapter 11

More Accusations

"No, don't..."

The painful whisper woke Jonathan from his uneasy sleep. He sat up wondering who had spoken. The room was filled with weird shadows shaped by the slivers of moonlight filtering through cracks in the canvas over the windows. In the corner behind the fire he could see a small group of young men fast asleep.

He turned over and closed his eyes. He must have been dreaming. But the floor was hard and unyielding and sleep refused to return. Instead he lay quite still, thinking.

"I want to go home..."

That wasn't his imagination.

Jonathan sat up with a rush and leaned over the inert body next to him. "Ben... Ben!" He shook him by the shoulder

Ben grunted, flung up an arm and turned to the right.

Jonathan prodded him in the back. "Wake up. You're having a nightmare. You're talking in your sleep."

There was a prickling silence as Ben pushed himself into a half-sitting position. He stared, bleary-eyed, at Jonathan. "What's goi... ohhh...!"

Jonathan raised an eyebrow. "Now what's wrong?"

"Nothing… sorry… yes… there is… I think I'm going to be sick."

"Not in here." Jonathan scrambled to his feet and pulled Ben up with him. "Come on. Let's get you outside."

With a muffled sob, Ben stumbled after him.

Jonathan reached the door first. He held it open until Ben was safely through. As the door swung closed he grabbed his arm and dragged him into the nearest barn. "Sit down and put your head between your knees," he ordered.

Ben shook his head. Instead he staggered into a corner and was violently sick.

Jonathan swallowed and turned away. For a moment he thought he would be sick as well. He peered out of the barn trying to block out the sounds of retching.

A sudden shout startled him. He half-turned. But the shout hadn't come from Ben. He was still doubled-up. Besides it was the wrong direction. "Try and make less noise," Jonathan whispered peering outside again. "Somebody's wandering around."

Ben straightened up. Leaning against the wall he closed his eyes. "What's that?" he said wiping his mouth on the back of his hand.

"Someone's walking around outside. The trouble is I don't know who it is. It might be Robert or possibly… the Bailiff."

Ben groaned. "The Bailiff – oh Jonathan, what am I going to do? I'm really scared."

For the first time since they'd met, Jonathan felt sorry for him. What would happen if Sir Henry believed the Bailiff and not Ben? What would happen to all of them?

The clatter of hooves rang through the compound making him jump. He stepped back hastily into the darkness of the barn as a troop of horses went by. "The King's bodyguard," he whispered over his shoulder.

"Really? Why are they up so early?"

"I don't know…" Jonathan moved closer to the door again. "There's two or three men by the gate. One's holding a horse. The King must be leaving… of course, that's it. Don't you remember, Robert said he was going to Lyndhurst – for the hunting?"

Ben walked unsteadily over to the door. "That means I'm in real trouble," he said, his face pinched and bleak in the breaking half-light. "Sir Henry is bound to want to see me after he's gone. What if he believes the Bailiff?"

"He won't." Jonathan was determined to sound positive even though his own stomach was churning. Suppose he was wrong? Suppose Sir Henry did agree with the Bailiff?

Ben stared at the waiting bodyguard. "You're right, he is going," he said in a half-whisper.

William Rufus mounted his horse and settled himself in the saddle. He raised his left arm. Sir Henry and his companion bowed. Opposite the barn the soldiers gathered up their reins and followed the King out of the compound.

As the last horse trotted through the gateway Sir Henry clapped the man beside him on the shoulder. They turned together and for a moment Jonathan relaxed. It wasn't the Bailiff after all… it was Robert. He was about to tell Ben the good news when a third person emerged from the shadows by the Hall.

He glanced at Ben who was staring, transfixed, at the familiar squat figure. "Are you thinking what I'm thinking?" Jonathan whispered as the three men entered the Hall.

"Probably… we should go in after them?"

Jonathan nodded. "Yes. We might as well get it over and done with."

"I guess you're right," Ben muttered leading the way across the compound.

Much to Jonathan's surprise the Hall was completely empty, except for the three men.

Sir Henry was leaning back in his chair listening to Robert who was standing behind him, next to the Bailiff.

Hearing the door creak Sir Henry looked up, saw Jonathan and Ben and beckoned. "Come over here." His voice rang up into the rafters.

Jonathan pushed Ben forward. "Don't worry," he whispered. "Remember I'm right behind you."

Ben smiled gratefully. At the foot of the dais he stopped in front of Sir Henry and bowed.

"My Bailiff tells me you are a thief. If you are, boy, the penalties are severe."

Jonathan shuddered.

"Well? What have you to say?" The impatient question filtered through the buzzing in Jonathan's ears.

"It's true that…"

Jonathan gasped. Robert hissed audibly. The Bailiff smirked.

Ben shook his head. "No… That's wrong… I didn't mean it to sound like that. What I was trying to say was – yes – it is true – the Bailiff did find me in the barn. But I wasn't taking anything. I am *not* a thief."

"Then why were you there?"

Ben hung his head. "I wanted to see if it had corn in it."

"He lies my Lord. Do not listen to him. These travellers have bewitched Master Robert. Now they are trying to use their witchcraft on you."

"That's nonsense," protested Jonathan.

"Silence!" Sir Henry continued studying Ben. "Why should I believe you?"

Ben raised his head. "Because Sire, you made us most welcome. You gave us food to eat; a place to sleep. I would never betray your kindness or dishonour my family in that way," he said proudly.

Jonathan blinked, amazed by this unexpected composure.

Sir Henry leaned across the table. "Why did you want to find out if there was corn in the barn?"

Ben grimaced. "The Bailiff had warned us we would not be allowed to finish work until all the corn in the compound had been bagged and taken to the mill. I was hungry. That's why I looked. I wanted to find out how much more there was to do."

"Hmm… is this true, Bailiff?"

The man ground his teeth. "Yes," he hissed.

Sir Henry studied Ben. "I believe my son may be right – that the three of you are honest folk… This time I will do nothing. But be warned… if Robert is proved wrong I will not hesitate to throw you and the rest of your family into prison."

"But… but… my Lord…"

"Enough Bailiff… no more. Come, it is time to select the best hides. My brother-in-law has advised me it is a good time to send our hides to Linhest. An excellent leather merchant is attending the market and he has arranged for him to see our goods."

Chapter 12
The Bailiff is Challenged

Early the following morning the wheels of a heavy coach rattled over cobblestones. It stopped by the front door of the Hall. Almost immediately Adela and her husband appeared, followed by Sir Henry and Lady Faversham, Robert, the Priest and a number of other members of the household. Sir Henry reached up and opened the door of the coach.

Adela turned to her mother, kissed her and then curtseyed to her father. In an instant he pulled her into his arms. "Take good care of my daughter," he growled glowering at his son-in-law over her head. "And remember, tonight you are to stay with my wife's brother in Linhest."

Adela's husband nodded. He turned to Lady Faversham, bowed low and raised her hand to his lips. Releasing it, he smiled at his bride and helped her into the coach. As he climbed in behind her, Sir Henry closed the door and clicked his fingers at the two men holding the horses' heads. They stepped back. The coachman half-stood and flicked his whip. Creaking loudly, the coach began to move, followed by a sturdy farm wagon packed with the bride's dowry.

Smiling, Adela leaned out of the window and waved.

She didn't stop until the coach had safely navigated the open gateway and started down the hill.

The convoy disappeared from sight.

Anxious to reach the forge before Conrad and get the fire going Jonathan said a quick goodbye to Victoria and Ben and left. Ben was less enthusiastic. Whatever he did he knew the miller would be only too ready to criticise so there wasn't much point in getting there early.

Victoria watched him walk away his shoulders hunched, his expression glum.

She felt sorry for him, but she also had a problem… Now that Adela had left she had no idea what she was supposed to do. Confused, she stood in the centre of the compound wondering who to ask. She had just decided to find Robert when she heard a voice she was beginning to hate.

"What do you think you're doing?"

She spun round.

"I said, what do you think you're doing?" the Bailiff snarled, podgy hands on hips.

"I don't know…"

"You don't know."

Stung by the sarcasm, Victoria flushed. "No… I don't. I was about to look for Robert. He might know what I'm meant to do now that Adela has left."

"It's Master Robert and Mistress Adela for the likes of you."

Victoria shrugged. "All right… Master Robert."

The Bailiff curled his lip. "You have no need to bother

the young Master. Where work is concerned I make the decisions. And I say you are to go into the fields with the other women."

Although the work was hard, it didn't take Victoria long to decide that building the sweet-smelling stooks of newly cut corn was greatly preferable to working in the dark and dismal confines of a stuffy hall. She paused when she'd finished making the third, mopped her brow and picked up a few long stalks. Twisting them into a crude rope she tied the fat bundle of corn and stood it against the other two. There, that was another done.

It was so peaceful out here. Yet there was so much to see. Rabbits bolting from the uncut corn whenever the reapers approached. Pigeons, cooing softly, feathers puffed up, strutting between the lengths of jagged stubble, grey heads bobbing up and down, beaks full of corn.

Not long after she'd arrived she'd caught a glimpse of a covey of partridges scurrying through the long grass at the edge of the field. Now she could see a red stag loping through the bracken on the other side of the river. Shading her eyes, Victoria stood and watched until it had join a small herd of deer lying half-hidden in the shade of a solitary oak tree. She smiled as it lay down, collected another bundle of straw and sniffed, enjoying the warm fruity smell.

But as the morning progressed and the sun continued to beat down on Victoria's neck trickles of sweat ran down her back, soaking her dress. Her head began to ache. Her hands were raw with burst blisters.

She began to feel sorry for herself, as she staggered across the field leaving a crazy line of tilting stooks behind. Once she shut her eyes, hoping to blot out the glare of the sun – but it was no good. It meant she couldn't see anything.

Her head buzzed. Squinting, she faltered looking for someone to help her. But there was no one. The other women had all moved on. She was completely on her own.

Without thinking she tried to run but, almost immediately, put her foot down a rabbit hole. She fell. Biting her lip she lay quite still as a searing pain shot up her left leg.

As her breathing began to ease she sat up with a groan. Rubbing her ankle she looked around wondering what she should do.

"Oi… you!"

She stared at the sturdy New Forest pony cantering towards her.

"You – what d'ya think yer doing?" The Bailiff yanked at the pony's mouth. It slowed down and he leaned over its shoulder his eyes fixed angrily on Victoria. He cracked his whip.

She screamed. Blood oozed from a cut on the back of her hand. She stared at it. "Why did you do that?" she whispered, her eyes full of pain.

The whip cracked again this time only missing her face because she ducked as the thong whistled past her left cheek. The pony shied. The Bailiff tightened his grasp on the reins. "Understand this – I will do anything – anything I want. *You* will do what I say. Right now I am ordering you to get up and start working."

Dusk began to fall. The faint chimes of the evening bell wafted across the valley. Around the open fields the workers straightened up, stretched their aching backs and gathered together their tools. One by one they set off to the nearest track. Her ankle and hand throbbing, her face scratched and tear-stained, Victoria limped along the rough path as best she could at the back of the line of women.

Jonathan leapt up when she entered the hall and beckoned. "Over here. We've saved you a place."

Ben slithered along the bench and patted the seat. "Sit down. You look exhausted."

"Are you all right?" Jonathan said, his expression concerned as she sat between them.

Victoria brushed away a tear.

"What's wrong?" Jonathan caught her left hand and squeezed sympathetically.

Victoria squealed.

Startled he looked down. "It wasn't that hard…" His eyes widened. "Oh… my… how did you do that?" He gazed at the angry weal crusted with dried blood.

Somebody laughed. Victoria glanced past his shoulder. The colour drained from her cheeks. She shivered.

Jonathan followed her gaze.

Three men were standing by the fire warming their backs and chatting – the Gleeman, Sir Henry and the Bailiff, the latter absent-mindedly running the thong of his whip between his thumb and finger.

An angry flush spread across Jonathan's thin cheeks. "He did it, didn't he?" he hissed.

Victoria bit her lip and nodded.

Ben leapt to his feet.

"Hey, what do you think you're doing?" Jonathan grabbed his tunic and dragged him back down on to the seat.

"Let go – damn you! Somebody's got to teach that man a lesson. First he beats me up. Now he's attacked Victoria."

"Well it's not going to be you." Jonathan released Ben and stood up. "You can't afford to get into more trouble."

Ben glared at him.

"Please Ben, Jonathan's right. Stay here and keep quiet. People are beginning to look… no Jonathan…" her voice rose shrilly, "…I don't want you to go, either."

"Sorry, but for once Ben is right. Something has got to be done about him. Don't worry. I'm not stupid. I won't go barging in shouting abuse. I'm going to speak to Robert."

"What do you think he's saying," Ben said watching Jonathan talking to Robert.

Victoria shrugged.

Robert glanced their way, said something and turned back to Jonathan, frowning.

"Well?" Ben said when Jonathan rejoined them.

"He said he'll sort it out."

A loud bang on the door of the hut woke the sleeping women. Yawning, Victoria dragged her dress over her head. She was tired and fed up. Her clothes were filthy. She knew she stank and needed a bath. Worse of all ahead of her lay another day in the fields.

Dejected, she joined the crowd of laughing, chattering women outside waiting for the day's orders. Silence fell when the Bailiff emerged. "Back to the fields," he shouted. "This time keep up with the men." He strutted up to Victoria and grabbed her arm. "Where do you think you are going," he whispered silkily in her ear.

Victoria swallowed. "I… I assumed you meant me as well," she said, keeping her eyes lowered.

"Why would you think that?" The Bailiff walked around her flexing his whip.

Mesmerized Victoria stared at the leather thong. She licked her lips. "I don't know," she said unhappily. "I just thought you meant me."

"Who told you to think?" the Bailiff sneered.

"What do you mean?"

"What do I mean? I mean you do not need to think – you need to do what I say. And I say – today you are not going into the fields. You are to help the swineherd."

"The swineherd?"

"Yes – the swineherd. Now, be off." The Bailiff cracked his whip.

Her sight blurred by a sudden rush of tears Victoria ran to the gate – and stopped. Determined not to let the odious man see she was crying she brushed away the unfallen tears before looking over her shoulder.

"NOW WHAT?" he yelled.

She took a deep breath. "I don't know where I'm going," she yelled back defiantly.

The Bailiff snorted. "Take the south path out of the village and keep walking." He grinned unpleasantly. "All you need do is follow your nose and you won't get lost."

Chapter 13

The Swineherd and His Mother

Victoria prodded the flimsy door. It immediately swung open and an overpowering stench hit her in the face. She backed away and it closed behind her.

With her hand pressed over her nose she pushed the door again and, holding her breath, peered inside the hut.

Waves of acrid smoke poured through the opening, engulfing Victoria, making it difficult for her to see. But as her eyes became used to the murkiness she realised with a start there was someone inside the hut. A stoutish woman, dressed in typical peasant garb had been sitting on a three-legged stool beside the fire until she saw Victoria. Then she stood up and waved the ladle she'd been using to stir the pot, threateningly. "Who be thee?"

Victoria blinked, taken aback.

"Well?"

"Er… sorry. I'm Victoria. The Bailiff sent me. He said I was to help the swineherd."

The woman snorted. "Huh! Wot be that dratted man thinking of? You… help my Alvin? We needs a man not a wench." She snorted again, her small eyes fixed on Victoria. When there was no response she shrugged her shoulders. "Oh, very well, I'll call him. But 'e won't be pleased."

Assuming rightly that Alvin must be the swineherd, Victoria let the woman pass, then followed her outside.

The woman nodded at a nearby bench. "Wait there," she ordered. Marching into the centre of the glade she stopped under a stout oak tree. "ALVIN," she roared.

Somewhere… deep in the forest Victoria thought she heard a faint squealing.

"ALVIN!"

There was still no reply. His mother glanced across at Victoria. "He must be too far away to hear. No matter! I can find you work… plenty of work. Come with me."

They hurried along the well-trodden path at the side of the hut to where a line of pens had been built at the edge of the forest. As she walked Victoria was pretty certain she could hear the telltale burble of water trickling over pebbles and rocks.

The woman stopped by the nearest pigsty and beckoned.

"How many pigs did you say there were?" Ben propped himself on his elbow and stared at Victoria curiously.

They were lying in a tangle of bracken on the hill behind the Hall waiting for the sun to set.

"I didn't. There were eight pens each with a sow that had recently farrowed and…" She blushed when she saw Jonathan frown. "Have I got that wrong?"

He smiled sadly. "No. We have pigs on the farm…" His voice tailed away.

"Oh… I'm so sorry… I didn't think… but it's what

Alvin's mother said. Oh Jonathan, you should have seen them… the piglets I mean. I never thought I'd say this but pigs can be quite sweet, can't they? One was covered in black spots – just like a Dalmatian puppy. Alvin's m…"

Ben prodded her. "Before you go any further who exactly is this Alvin?"

"Sorry… didn't I say… the swineherd. Can you imagine – he's lived in that hut by the forest all his life. I didn't meet him today but his mother promised to make sure he stayed around tomorrow until I get there."

"Where was he?" Ben nibbled a blade of grass thoughtfully.

"In the forest… with the rest of the herd. He takes them out at sunrise and doesn't get back until dusk."

Ben plucked another blade of grass. "Why?"

"He has to stay with them. They're not his. According to his mother he'd be in real trouble if any got lost. Most belong to Sir Henry, but a few people like the Bailiff and Priest own some."

"What about this Alvin?"

"What about him?"

"Doesn't he have any pigs?"

"Oh… I see what you mean. Yes… three sows."

"And what did you have to do?" Jonathan asked, changing the subject.

Victoria wrinkled her nose. "She made me muck out the pens… which was pretty disgusting. Then I had to collect some acorns to feed…"

"Acorns!"

Victoria stared in surprise at Jonathan. "Yes – acorns – they're fed to the pigs."

Ben's eyes sparkled with excitement. "I get it… acorns!"

"What's going on? I know I'm being dim, but would one of you please explain?"

"I'd have thought it was obvious." Jonathan grinned. "Especially as you found the clue."

"The clue?" Victoria frowned. Her mouth fell open. She clapped her hand to her forehead. "Of course… why didn't I think of that? How stupid! Acorns! What should we do?"

"We're not doing anything… you are. You have to find out if Alvin knew Edgar," said Ben.

"He couldn't have." Victoria shook her head decisively.

It was Ben's turn to frown. "You can't know that. You haven't even met him yet."

"I might not have met him but I've met his mother. She's not much older than my mum."

"So what?"

Jonathan grimaced. "Don't be stupid, Ben. Can't you see what Victoria is saying? Alvin wouldn't have been born when Edgar was alive."

She nodded.

"I can see it makes it more difficult… but what Ben said does make sense," Jonathan continued thoughtfully. "Edgar must have gone there sometimes."

"I don't see why."

"Okay… try this for an idea. We agreed, didn't we, that Edgar was probably the last person to have had the Sun?"

Victoria and Ben nodded.

"What if he knew he was going to die?"

Victoria looked a little doubtful. "It still doesn't explain why he hid it."

"Doesn't it? I disagree. He'd have known it was important… very important."

"Of course… you're right," Ben said excitedly. "My dad told me the Star was important when he gave it to me. I bet you anything he was told the same thing."

It was Victoria's turn to grimace. "If Edgar hid the Sun – why on earth did he leave all these clues?"

Jonathan shook his head. "That I'm… er… not sure of," he said conscious of this weakness in his theory.

"I've an idea," said Ben. He looked embarrassed as the others stared at him.

"Well?" said Victoria.

"If Edgar knew the Sun was important he might have thought someone would be sent to find it when they learned he had died. If they were then they'd need those clues."

Jonathan and Victoria looked at each other, then at Ben, puzzled.

"Well someone must know about the talismans – as well as us I mean," he said defiantly.

There was a long silence, then Victoria said: "Sylvene knows about them, she told me."

"Yes…" said Jonathan remembering the mirror. "The jewellers who made them would also have known about them… and our parents. In fact, if you think about it, there are probably loads of people who know about the talismans. If Ben's right about the clues and I think he is… we need to discover how Edgar is linked to acorns."

"And that brings us right back to finding out if he used to visit the swineherd."

Jonathan laughed. "You've got it, Victoria."

"Except he couldn't have, remember?"

A strained silence fell over them. Ben was the first to break it. "Does it have to be Alvin? What about his mother?"

Jonathan's eyes widened. "You've got it, Ben. If Alvin's about our age Edgar would have known his mother."

"You're telling me I've got to build a sty?"

The young man standing at the far end of the row of pens grinned at Victoria's protest. Tall, with shoulder length blond hair, a short neat beard and piercing blue eyes, the swineherd was a little older than she'd expected. Even so, it was quite apparent that he was far too young to have known Edgar.

Alvin picked up a stake. "Don't you worry, Mistress. I will help. Furst we need one more post." Humming softly he hammered the stake into the ground. "See – the beginning of the frame. Now all we need are the walls." He selected a split length of hazel from the bundle by his feet. "T'is easy – jest you watch." As he spoke he was weaving the hazel between the stakes, bending it slightly at every post. When that length ran out he grabbed another and handed it to Victoria. "You try."

She grinned at him and took the strip of hazel. By the time she'd finished weaving it between the posts her hands were hurting; but she was so pleased with her achievement she didn't seem to notice. Instead she reached for a second length and continued working.

Alvin smiled and selected one himself. They worked steadily on opposite sides of the pen until all three walls were complete. Then, leaving Victoria to make the run, Alvin began thatching the roof of the sty.

They were working on a second new sty when Victoria noticed Alvin's mother approaching. She stood up. Wincing, she arched her back.

The woman smiled sympathetically. "T'is hard work," she said. "Would you like something to drink?"

Victoria licked her lips and nodded.

"Wait here. I will fetch water."

She bustled away. Victoria glanced at her companion. "Alvin, if you and your mother are here today who's looking after the herd?"

"A lad from the village." He shook his head and rapped the top of her fence. "Too many holes. Piglets will find it easy to escape through them."

"'Ave done Alvin, 'ave done. Victoria is weary," protested his mother overhearing this criticism on her return. She handed Victoria an earthen jug. "Drink deeply! You will be better fer it."

Alvin snorted and turned on his heel.

Victoria wiped her mouth on her sleeve. "Where's he going? He's not cross, is he?"

"Nah… he's off to the coppice – fer more hazel. He'll be back quick enuf!" She crouched beside Victoria. "Don't tell him I said so – but he's right, lass. You must fill the gaps. Here – let me show you."

By the time Alvin returned with a bundle of sticks strapped to his back Victoria was alone, working on the second side of the pen. He undid the strap and dropped the bundle on the ground. "Better," he said grudgingly glancing at the fence and then at Victoria. Turning away he spat in the palms of his hands, selected a stick and picked up his axe.

One blow split the hazel lengthways. Alvin tossed the two pieces on the ground. "It is hot, too hot," he grumbled picking up another stick. He glanced skywards. "Too hot…"

A clap of thunder rolled around the tops of the trees.

There was a shocked gasp.

Victoria looked up. Alvin was standing, wide-eyed and rigid, his face ashen staring at a sheet of lightning that was ripping the clouds apart. There was a second, louder rumble of thunder. With a terrified shout Alvin flung aside his axe and fled.

Alvin's mother dragged a stool closer to the fire and pushed Victoria on to it. "Sit, girl and get warm. You be wet through. Whatever were yer thinking, son, keeping her working out in all that rain."

"We weren't working." Victoria held out her hands to the fire. "We got wet just coming here." She blushed aware that the woman was watching her curiously. "Er... have you always lived here?" she said saying the first thing that came into her mind.

"I have." Another log went on to the fire. "Me father was swineherd and his father afore him. And when me father died the Lord made me husband swineherd."

"Oh... yes... I remember... you said. Don't you get lonely out here? Wouldn't you like to live in the village?"

The woman chuckled. "Live in the village. Nay lass. Who would look after the pigs? 'Tis too far to walk them everyday from the village to the forest. Besides – I like it here. We have all we need – the brook fer water, a place to sleep, a bit of land fer our food, roots and acorns a-plenty fer the pigs."

Acorns.

Victoria's eyes lit up.

"And if you want a chat, why there's allus folk coming out wanting to see if their pigs be ready. There's the Bailiff and Master Robert..."

"Robert?"

Alvin's mother curled her lip. "Yes, Sir Henry sends him – when he wants us ter kill a pig."

"Oh! Is that what the previous... the Saxon Lord... did? Did he come... or... or did he send Edgar to tell you when to kill a pig?"

The woman threw up her hands. "Oh my! Oh my!

'Ow that name do bring back memories. Wherever did you hear tell about Edgar?"

"From the blacksmith."

"Conrad!" The woman's eyes twinkled. "Now he were a handsome lad – make no mistake."

"But what about Edgar?" Victoria persisted. "Did you know him?"

"Oh yes. He were lovely. So kind and clever." Her smiled faded. She sighed. "Ah his poor mother. I were naught but a lass when he died. It were a great loss."

"Why did he come?"

Alvin's mother shrugged off her sadness. The twinkle crept back into her eyes. "Fer a bit o' company. We'd walk in the forest and he'd tell me all about Lunnon. A huge city he did say. A place where hundreds of folk live side by side. Yes, Victoria, I knows it is hard to believe but that were what Edgar told me and he were never a liar. Sometimes he would bring his harp here and play fer us."

Victoria gasped.

The woman looked at her in surprise. "He were good at that," she insisted.

That evening, after the meal, Jonathan, Ben and Victoria huddled together in a corner of the Hall watching the troupe of jugglers who had arrived that morning, perform.

"So what else did she tell you?" whispered Ben.

"There wasn't time for anything else. The rain stopped. We had to go back to work."

"But there are acorns out there?" said Jonathan.

"Loads."

"That settles it. We'll have to go and see what we can find." Jonathan grinned. "How about Sunday? No one would notice if we skipped church."

Chapter 14
Deciphering Sylvene

"Do you think Sylvene is actually trying to get us out of here?"

Jonathan and Victoria stared at Ben.

"Well," he said defensively. "You have to admit nothing seems to be happening."

It was early on Sunday morning. Hoping to slip away unnoticed, they were waiting quietly in the compound as the stream of villagers poured down the hill to the church. When the last person disappeared from sight they set off themselves.

The sun beat warmly on their heads as they entered the village. Seagulls circled overhead, keening plaintively. In single file they walked along the main street which led to the river. But when the bridge came in sight instead of continuing towards it, they took the fork to the right. This led them away from the river and circled a field of corn waiting to be cut. Before long, clumps of encroaching bracken together with straggling brakes of gorse swamped the grass on either side of the path.

They'd been walking in silence for sometime when Jonathan said unexpectedly: "I'm bothered about Sylvene."

"What?" Victoria wrinkled her nose. "Why are you

bothered… oh… I see what you mean…"

"I don't," said Ben.

"It's just that there are so many unanswered questions. Questions like – do any of us really know her – did she have something to do with what happened at the Rufus Stone? Did she know we were going to go back in time?"

"She must have, otherwise she couldn't have shown herself to me like that in the mirror."

"That's right. Don't you think we should tell each other everything we do know about her?"

"Mmm…"

Jonathan glanced at Ben. "How about you starting?"

Ben grimaced. "Er… okay… I suppose so. Let's see… why don't I begin with the really obvious? Her name is Sylvene Baker and… *now* what?" he exclaimed hearing a sharp intake of breath.

"She's not Sylvene Baker, she's Sylvene Browne," said Jonathan.

Victoria shook her head. "You're both wrong. She's Sylvene Dunbar."

Ben scratched his head. "What's going on? This doesn't make much sense…"

"It doesn't, does it?" Jonathan said wearily. "That's the trouble. Nothing seems to make sense anymore. Okay Ben, just tell us what you do know about her. We'll try and sort it out later."

"Well… she's a member of my Dad's research team at Bristol. The rest of the team think she's a bit of a workaholic. She's too keen. Sometimes she comes here by herself. That was why I thought she'd deliberately chosen the campsite in the New Forest, remember?"

Jonathan and Victoria nodded.

"It's the sort of thing she'd do. She's not fashion conscious… she never worries about what she's wearing… just wants to get on with her work. I suppose that's not really so surprising. You get filthy when you're excavating…"

The hair on the back of Jonathan's neck prickled. Ben's Sylvene didn't sound a bit like the one he knew. He forced himself to concentrate.

"…and that's really all I know about her. What about you, two?"

"I'm completely confused," Jonathan said slowly.

"Why?"

"So many of the things you told us about her are wrong I hardly recognise her. Take the name. As I said, my Sylvene is Sylvene Browne, not Baker. And she's always immaculate. I can't remember ever seeing her look untidy, even when she's gardening. As for wearing something dirty… impossible. She doesn't work, she travels a lot…"

"How did you meet her?" interrupted Victoria.

"She bought the derelict windmill down the lane from our farm about four or five years ago. She had builders in to renovate it and didn't move in until they'd finished, about six months later.

"Jenny, my kid sister, was riding home from a gymkhana

117

one Saturday afternoon when something startled her pony outside her front gate. He shied. She fell off and rolled into a bed of nettles. We didn't know there'd been an accident until Jacko charged, riderless, into the farmyard. Dad grabbed his keys from the dairy but before he'd reached the Landover a car drove into the yard."

Jonathan grinned. "I can still see him, all overalls and wellies, yelling for Mum, as he lugged Jenny up to the house. Behind him Sylvene was picking her way between the cowpats in a pair of gold-spangled sandals. Luckily Jenny was okay – just a few bruises and a nasty attack of nettle rash. When everyone had calmed down Sylvene introduced herself. After that she was always popping in. It wasn't long before it felt as though we'd known her all the time. She was part of the family."

Victoria frowned. "What else?"

Jonathan thought for a moment. "She goes away quite often. When she comes back the first thing she does is stop at the farm for a cup of tea with Mum," he grinned, "and to catch up on the gossip."

"It's still not a lot. Can't you think of anything – anything at all that might help?" said Victoria. "You said she doesn't work. Does she have a boyfriend?"

"Not that I know of – but that doesn't mean anything. She might be going to see a boyfriend when she goes away."

"Okay! Let's go over everything. You keep saying she goes away a lot. Where does she go?"

Jonathan shrugged. "I've never bothered to ask. It

could be France. She speaks excellent French – which is why she gets on so well with Mum. I'm sorry, Victoria, I know it's pretty feeble but I really can't think of anything else that might help. What about you?"

Victoria sighed. "All right, let's see. Sylvene is more a friend of the family than my friend. She was introduced to us as Sylvene Dunbar and lives in a house in our street. She joined the local painting club which is where she met my Mum.

"I've stayed with her a couple of times when Mum and Dad have gone away. She's fun; likes doing crazy things like paddling in the Serpentine or roller-blading in Hyde Park. I'm pretty certain she's a courier for a travel agency because, you're right Jonathan she does go away a lot and when she comes home she usually brings a foreign doll for my collection."

"And…?" demanded Jonathan as she fell silent.

It was Victoria's turn to look confused. "It's odd… but when I think about it… there really isn't much else to tell," she said at last.

They walked on each lost in their own thoughts until Ben broke the silence. "How much farther before we get to this pig-place?"

"Not far. In fact…" Victoria touched his arm and pointed, "…do you see that smoke?" He nodded. "That's where we're going."

Jonathan stepped in front of them and turned barring the way. "I've just thought of something else…"

"Now what? I'm thirsty," complained Ben.

Jonathan ran the chain around his neck between his fingers. "Sorry, but this is important. I think Sylvene knew about our talismans when she invited us on holiday."

Victoria and Ben glanced at each other, but kept quiet; as though realising that Jonathan needed time... time to talk through his thoughts.

"If she did," he continued softly, "it would mean she was definitely involved in our coming here... No... that's wrong... she wasn't involved... she set it up. That's awful. She must have been planning it for ages; possibly from the day we first met her; or even before. Don't you see? It could explain the different lives and..."

"Surnames," said Victoria reaching out to him.

He smiled weakly and nodded. "Yes... surnames. I've never met anyone before with three different surnames – have you?"

They shook their heads.

"Of course not. Nobody would do that unless they were hiding something. Think back to when this started... the first day of the holiday. Remember the clouds – the ones heading for the coast? I swear they changed course. It was rain from them that drove the tourists from the Rufus Stone. *That* must be when it happened.

"Victoria, after Ben left, you said the coaches had gone as well. Then we noticed there weren't any cars in the car park. Now think! Do you actually remember seeing the car park?"

Victoria frowned. She shook her head. "No," she said slowly. "What's more I can't remember seeing the Rufus Stone either."

"Couldn't it just be a coincidence?" asked Ben.

Jonathan looked at him. "There are too many coincidences. For instance none of us had met each other before this holiday. Yet we each own a talisman. It was Sylvene who brought us together. The key has to be her. "

They walked to the edge of the glade. Victoria stopped. "Right," she said. "Over there is the hut but before we find Alvin I just want to make one thing clear – I'm going to do the talking."

Jonathan and Ben nodded.

"Good." Victoria picked up her skirts. Running to the hut she pushed open the door and stepped inside.

Ben peered over her shoulder. "Pooh, it really does pong. You weren't exaggerating. Where do you think they are?"

"I've no idea. We'll try the pigpens." She darted around the side of the hut, clapped her hands and pointed. A figure was sweeping leaves into small heaps. "I was right," Victoria crowed.

Hearing a shout, Alvin's mother stopped working and stood quite still, her eyes flitting from Jonathan to Ben.

"It's all right – they're with me," Victoria called seeing her worried expression.

"Good… good. It jest shook me a little… we don't get many strangers out here."

"Sorry… I should have told you I was bringing them.

They're my brothers."

"Ah!" Alvin's mother relaxed and smiled at Jonathan.

He beamed back. "Yes, my little sister," he patted Victoria's head, "told us so much about your pigs we wondered if you'd show them to us," he continued ignoring Victoria's glare.

"I'm sorry young master, my son has taken the herd into the forest but you are most welcome to take a look at the sows. I doubt you will have seen their like before."

She propped the broom against the side of the nearest pen, picked up a bucket and rattled the handle. A black snout appeared above the fence and sniffed.

Alvin's mother threw a handful of acorns into the pen and a stream of piglets tumbled out of the sty. Squealing and snorting they rooted amongst the leaves.

"They're grand." Jonathan leaned over the wattle fence and scratched the sow behind the ears. "Victoria tells us you have a large herd."

The woman cast him an uneasy look.

"Honestly Jonathan! Don't you ever listen? I said most of the pigs belong to Sir Henry..."

"Victoria is right. We own but three pigs. A few belong to villagers – like the Priest. The rest are Sir Henry's."

"Does Conrad have any?" Victoria asked innocently.

Jonathan shot her an appreciative look.

The woman nodded. "This sow and another – but 'er's out with Alvin – in the forest." She put down the bucket, grabbed the broom and began sweeping again.

"Jonathan's lucky. He works for Conrad."

The woman glanced up.

"Yes, I do," said Jonathan, wondering what on earth Victoria was up to now. "He's a good blacksmith."

"That's not all he is," continued Victoria cheerfully. She smiled at Alvin's mother. "Did you know he liked carving?"

Bemused, the woman shook her head.

"Oh, you must have seen them at the forge! Why the front of the porch is covered in them…"

"No Victoria, you've got it wrong," Jonathan said quickly. "I never said Conrad carved them."

"Oh, I thought you did."

"No. Different people did them. The miller was one. The son of the last Saxon Lord was another… now what did Conrad say his name was?"

"Edgar," said Alvin's mother.

Jonathan beamed. "That's right. And I remember what he carved… a harp."

"A harp… fancy that. Mind you it don't surprise me.'E loved his harp. Sometimes he'd bring it with him when he came to see us."

"Really?"

"Yes. If it were wet he would play it in the hut. But if the night were warm and peaceful like, we would sit on that old bench by the door while he sat under the oak, and played fer us…"

"How much longer are we staying here?" demanded Ben.

Jonathan glared. "There's no need to be rude."

"I'm not. I'm tired. You can stay if you want. I'm going

to find somewhere to sit. What about you, Victoria?"

She shot Jonathan an anxious look.

"Oh go with him. I won't be long. I'd just like to take a look at a couple more of these fine pigs."

"Did I give you enough time?" Jonathan asked as soon as they were some distance away from the swineherd's hut.

Victoria's eyes sparkled. She did a little jig. "Tell him, Ben. Tell him what we found."

"All right… all right. Calm down. We think we found the next clue."

"Don't be so modest. It was you. You found it."

"I don't care who found it… just tell me what it is."

"A cross," said Ben. "There was a cross almost halfway up the trunk of the oak tree."

"He's being modest," Victoria said excitedly. "There was so much ivy I thought there was no way we'd find anything. But Ben refused to give up. I was afraid we were going to be caught and then we found it…"

"A cross?" Jonathan asked.

"Yes. Do you think it stands for the church?" said Victoria.

"It could do. That's what they use on maps," said Jonathan.

"I know." Victoria grinned at him. "It's good, isn't it? Shall we go and have a look?"

Chapter 15
The Church

Robert stood at the foot of the narrow path that led up to the compound, fiddling with the hilt of his dagger. He'd been about to go and find Jonathan when his father had sent for him. He frowned. Nothing unusual had happened that day so what did his father want? He sighed. There was only one way to find out, he thought and started up the path. But he hadn't gone very far when he stopped again and looked down into the village.

Nothing moved. The streets were empty, so were the tiny gardens. Robert wasn't surprised. After the Sunday service all the villagers, except for the indoor servants, had gone out to the fields. Only the harvest mattered at this time of year. So, why did he feel uneasy?

He glanced up the hill. The gates of the compound were wide open. A cart came out. It turned to the left and made its way slowly down the wider track that led to the bottom of the valley and the cornfields. Robert grinned. He was being stupid. There was nothing to worry about.

He set off again but had only taken a few paces when he thought he heard a shout. He hesitated. Was it his imagination or was that laughter? He held his breath and listened. It was definitely laughter... floating up the side of the valley on a light breeze. He scanned the main street and smiled. Three figures were walking down the middle, laughing and chatting.

Robert was about to call out when they turned off the track and walked up the path to the church. A shiver ran down his spine as they went inside. He chewed his lower lip. Why had they gone into the church?

Without thinking, he plunged back down the hill, leaving a trail of dust rising into the air in his haste. At the porch, he paused, suddenly unsure what to do next. Suppose they only wanted to be somewhere quiet? Perhaps he should leave them to their meditation? He was turning away when a loud burst of laughter wafted across the churchyard.

A wave of fury swept over him. Clenching his fists he flung himself at the door and almost fell into the porch, startling Victoria who was bending over something in one of the corners.

She looked up. "Robert!" Her voice shook. "Oh... thank goodness it's you."

"Why? Who were you afraid it was?" he said his voice harsh.

"No one..." she held out her hand ready to help him to his feet.

He brushed it away.

Victoria frowned. "What's wrong?"

"Wrong? Wrong? How can you ask me that? Something is very wrong," said Robert getting to his feet. He grabbed her wrist pinching the skin between his thumb and forefinger until the tears sprang into her eyes.

"Stop it," she squealed trying to prise open his fingers with her free hand. "Let go. You're hurting."

"No," Robert yelled back. "Not until we have joined your friends." He wrenched open the door to the church and saw Jonathan, standing by the altar, the gold cross in his hand. Horrified, Robert flung Victoria aside sending her flying into a stone pillar.

"Thieves!"

The furious shout bounced off the back wall of the church.

Jonathan spun round. Alarmed, Ben stepped out of the south transept and stared.

"Thieves," Robert shouted again and pulled the dagger from its sheath. "The Bailiff was right. Yes, he was right. I was the fool... a complete fool. I should have listened to him; followed his advice; not been persuaded by your honeyed words. But I will make amends – DO NOT MOVE."

"Robert... look at Victoria... we can't just leave her lying there..."

"I say we can." Robert glanced at Victoria then back to Jonathan. "She is alive. I can see her breathing."

Victoria moved her legs a little and groaned.

"See, I said she was all right," Robert said flatly.

Very slowly Victoria pushed herself into a sitting position. "My head, oh my head," she moaned softly, clutching it with both hands as she leaned against the back wall.

"Robert if you're not going to help her, I am." His

eyes dark with anger Jonathan raced the length of the nave. But before he could reach Victoria Robert jumped in front of him, his dagger raised threateningly.

"I said, leave her. She is lucky. If I had my sword instead of my dagger Victoria would be dead by now. In fact, none of you would leave here alive."

Behind him Victoria struggled to her feet. Sensing the movement Robert half-turned and glared at her. "Neither of you move…"

"I don't intend to." Wincing with pain, Victoria felt the crown of her head. "There's a huge lump just here and my knee hurts… Robert, what do you think you're doing?" she said with an uneasy laugh as he grabbed her.

He held the dagger to her throat and looked over her shoulder at Jonathan and Ben: "You two, stay where you are if you want her to live."

Victoria twisted her head and glanced at him sadly. "Now you *are* being ridiculous," she said her face pale, her voice strained. She pushed the dagger away. "Stop being such an idiot and do us all a favour… explain what exactly it is we've done to upset you."

"I was a fool but my eyes have been opened," Robert said bitterly. "I can see you all for what you really are… The Bailiff saw it the day you arrived in our village. Thieves! You are nothing but thieves."

Victoria stared at him. "But I don't understand. What makes you think we're thieves?"

Robert pointed at the cross in Jonathan's hand. "What else can I believe?"

"This is ridiculous." Victoria stamped her foot and collapsed to the floor. "Ouch... now look what you made me do." She rubbed her knee and glared at Robert.

"Me?" He stared at her bemused.

"Yes you... don't look at me like that." She hauled herself up. "If you hadn't made me so angry I wouldn't have stamped my foot." Her lips twitched. She began to giggle. "The trouble is when I get mad I do things without thinking." She touched Robert lightly on his arm. "Please listen... we are not thieves, honestly. Take the cross and put it back on the altar. No one will try to stop you."

Robert held out his hand.

Jonathan gave him the cross and moved out of the way.

Robert stared at him contemptuously. Very deliberately he walked up to the altar and placed the cross on it. He backed away, paused and bowed.

Victoria let out a long sigh and clutched at a nearby pillar for support.

Jonathan glanced at her white face. "Are you all right?"

She nodded. "Yes. My head aches and my knee hurts but I'll be fine, honestly. Don't you think it's about time we told him everything?"

"I think you're right. We don't want him thinking we're thieves," Jonathan said.

"Hang on..." Ben shook his head. "Let's think about this first. We don't want to rush things... I'm not even sure he'll believe us if we tell him the truth. I know I wouldn't."

Victoria glanced at him, surprised. "What's the alternative?"

"Ssh… he's coming," Ben said.

They watched the taut figure approach.

Jonathan grimaced. "He doesn't look very happy, does he?"

Robert stopped in front of Victoria, his fingers playing with the hilt of the dagger now back in its sheath. "Come with me," he said, his voice strained, his expression grim.

"Where?" Jonathan asked slowly.

Robert glared at him. "To find my father, of course; he must decide what to do with you."

"No, Robert. First you must hear what we've got to say," Victoria said quickly.

"There's something we need to tell you…"

"We haven't agreed that, Victoria," Ben said angrily. "I don't think we should tell him anything. I don't trust him… not in this mood."

"Ben! How can you? After everything he has done – for you in particular." Victoria sounded shocked. "Who stood up for you when the Bailiff caught you in the barn? Who persuaded Sir Henry…"

"All right… all right. There's no need to go on… I've got the message," Ben said wriggling uneasily. "I take it all back. Go on. Tell him everything. Just don't blame me if it all goes horribly wrong."

"I won't… because it won't." Victoria crossed her fingers behind her back.

Robert glanced from her to Ben then across at Jonathan. "I do not understand. What do you want to tell me?"

"The truth," Victoria turned her back on Ben, "about us."

"The truth? Mon dieu…" Robert pointed at Jonathan, "…how can I believe anything you say after finding him stealing the cross?"

"That's not true, Robert. I wasn't stealing it. Can't you try and forget what you saw until we've explained?"

"Very well." Robert folded his arms and waited, his eyes hard and fixed on Jonathan.

Jonathan took a deep breath. "Could we go outside?"

"Outside… you do take me for a fool." Robert almost snorted. "Once we are outside the three of you will try to escape."

"No, we won't. You have my word on that."

A look of contempt flashed in Robert's eyes. "Your word… pah… take that for your word." He flicked his fingers in Jonathan's face.

Jonathan swallowed. "Yes, my word," he repeated his face suddenly very white.

"Why do you want us to go outside?"

"Because out there we're less likely to be interrupted."

Robert grabbed Victoria's wrist. "Very well." He rested his other hand on the hilt of his dagger. "Victoria and I will lead the way. But you must be quick. I am anxious to find my father… to tell him about your treachery." His eyes darkened with fury and he dragged Victoria towards the door.

Chapter 16
The Truth

Robert stormed outside pulling Victoria along with him.

She gasped as she stumbled awkwardly and her legs became tangled in her skirt. "Robert... you've got to slow down."

"No..." he hesitated as he glanced over his shoulder and saw that Jonathan and Ben had fallen some distance behind. His eyes cold, his gaze unwavering he glared at Victoria. "Very well, we will wait here," he said.

Thankfully she leaned against the rough wall of the church and began untangling her skirt. Hearing voices, she looked up. As she smiled at Jonathan and Ben Jonathan reached out his hand to her.

Robert brushed it away. "Victoria, are you ready? And you two, make sure you keep up this time." He walked diagonally across the churchyard towards a rickety gate none of them had ever noticed before.

They waited in silence as he climbed through the broken bars. Turning back to them he beckoned.

"This looks like a good place," Jonathan said standing in the middle of a sea of bracken. Although the tips of the ferns were beginning to turn brown the air was cool and fresh.

"It's not quiet enough," Robert said shortly. "Anyone

entering the churchyard would be able to hear us even if they couldn't see us. Over there," he pointed at a small thicket to their left, "that's where we're going."

He led them through the undergrowth surrounding the copse and then in amongst the trees. Dappled light streamed between gaps in the leaves, lightening the atmosphere.

But as they went further in the trees became thicker. The light grew dim and the air damp. Soon the bracken began to disappear beneath the creeping tentacles of a strange straggling plant that wound itself around the base of any tree or bush in the way.

"This will do." Robert pointed at a fallen tree. "Sit there."

Jonathan, Victoria and Ben did as they were told and waited, watching him warily.

Robert stared back, his expression stern. He knew they were waiting for him to speak. Obstinately, he made them wait even longer. He studied each in turn – Jonathan so cool, Victoria pale but determined, Ben scowling at nothing.

He felt betrayed. He had come to think of these travellers as his friends. Now he knew them for what they really were… nothing but a bunch of thieves. He clenched his fists. "Say what you have to say… but be quick." His tone was sharp and uninviting.

Jonathan nudged Victoria.

She shook her head. "You explain," she said.

"All right." Jonathan straightened his shoulders. "It's like this, Robert…"

"I do not understand," Robert complained breaking the silence that had fallen over them when Jonathan finished talking. He looked away, conscious they expected some kind of reaction. "I do not understand," he repeated and shook his head, annoyed for sounding so uncertain.

"Can you tell me what's worrying you?" Jonathan said.

The angry glint in Robert's eyes had been replaced by a puzzled look. He scratched his head. "I do not understand any of it. None of it makes sense. You tell me you are not from our time; that you have... how did you say it...? '*Come back*' from another time. Surely that is nonsense?"

"You'd think so but I'm afraid it's not," said Victoria.

"It is all so... so confusing!" The word exploded from his lips.

"But it's all true," Victoria said quickly.

Robert shook his head. "How can I believe you?" he said.

Jonathan and Ben looked at each other helplessly.

"I'll try and make it clearer," Victoria said. She frowned. "I think we have to go back to the day we arrived."

He nodded.

"Do you remember what we were wearing?"

Robert frowned. "Why do you ask?"

"Because it's important. Your father thought we were wearing some kind of costume."

He nodded. "That's right. You said you'd been left in the forest by a troupe of players who..."

"We did… but there never was a troupe. Jonathan made it up…"

"He did what?" Robert glared at Jonathan.

"He had to… it was the only thing he could think of at the time that would explain our clothes. Robert, what we were wearing is not unusual. Most of our friends in the twenty-first century wear jeans."

"Jeans… twenty-first century." Robert shook his head. "Victoria, women do not wear such things. It is not seemly. They must be costumes."

Victoria grinned. "Girls of my age never wear skirts if they can help it. They prefer jeans or trousers…"

Robert blinked at yet another strange word. "Trousers?"

"Yes, trousers!" She pointed at his leggings. "Trousers are a little like those except they hang loose."

"And you say women wear these… these trousers?" She nodded.

"My mother would not approve." Robert rubbed his forehead distractedly. He glanced at Jonathan and changed the subject to one he felt would be safer. "If you are not from my time how did you get here?"

There was an awkward silence. Jonathan looked at Victoria who shrugged. "It's your turn," she said.

He turned to Ben who immediately stared at his feet. "Thanks," he said cynically. "Robert, the trouble is we don't really know. One moment we were reading the inscription on the Rufus Stone, the next…"

"Nothing," Victoria joined in, "absolutely nothing. No cars; no coaches; no Rufus Stone; no Sylvene."

Robert blinked. "Cars? Coa… Coa…"

"Coaches." Ben grinned.

"Coaches…" Robert let the word roll off his tongue. He glanced at Jonathan. "But these words mean nothing to me. What are they?"

Jonathan pulled a wry face. "A car is sort of like a horse and cart – except there isn't a horse and they go much faster."

An angry flush spread over Robert's cheeks. "No horse… do you take me for a fool? How can a cart move without a horse?"

"Believe me, they can in our time."

"Why should I?" Robert's voice was shaking with rage. There was another tense silence. Then he let out a low sigh and smiled a small, edgy smile. "I am sorry. Please forget what I said. I did not mean it. Tell me… tell me about this Rufus Stone. I have never heard of such a thing. It must be very precious. Is the stone used by alchemists?"

"No. It's not that kind of stone," said Jonathan.

"It's more of a monument," said Ben.

Jonathan glared. Victoria gasped. Her hand flew to her mouth.

Robert turned to her. "Why do you look like that? What does 'monument' mean?"

She shook her head.

"I'll tell you," said Ben. "They're usually put somewhere

to remind people of something that happened there."

"Why is it called a Rufus Stone?"

Victoria shrugged. "Goodness knows…" She glared at Ben who coloured.

"Oh!" Robert frowned, his mind racing. There were so many questions he wanted to ask but he didn't know where to begin. He decided to go back to the very beginning. "Did you really say that you don't know how you came to my time?"

Jonathan nodded. "We didn't even know we'd gone back."

"Truly?"

"Truly." Jonathan smiled uncertainly. "Well, not until we got here… though I have to admit there were some signs that we missed…"

"Signs… what kind of… signs?"

"Well – like the hunt we saw in the Forest…"

"And the French." Ben shuddered. "That was really scary… like being in a never-ending French lesson."

"Or going on an exchange trip," suggested Victoria, giggling at his expression.

"An exchange trip?" Robert raised his eyebrows.

"French isn't that difficult," Jonathan said.

"Not for you… with your French grandparents," said Ben. "Mine is awful… You can't imagine how hard it's been for me – having to speak it all the time."

Bewildered, Robert turned to Ben. "Why? What do you speak?"

"English of course."

"English?" His face cleared. "Oh, you mean Saxon."

"No I do not. Saxon is worse than French. I mean English."

Robert shook his head. "It is too difficult," he complained, struggling with his thoughts. "What did you do when you realised what had happened?"

"We didn't know what to do." Victoria rested her elbows on her knees and cupped her chin in the palms of her hands. "How could we? We didn't even know why we were here."

"That must have been terrible." Robert smiled more sympathetically. "When did you find out?"

"It sort of happened. Discovering we each had a talisman was a help."

"So was Sylvene when she appeared in that mirror," said Jonathan.

"Ah yes... Sylvene. Tell me more about her."

Jonathan grimaced. "There isn't a lot to tell..."

"There must be," said Robert.

"I'd say the one real thing we've discovered since we've been here is that we don't know anything about Sylvene," Ben said. "How could we when she claims to be three different people?"

"Three different people... Ben, that is ridiculous. Nobody can be three different people."

"I know that. You know that. Apparently Sylvene doesn't know that."

Victoria gave a short laugh. "It's all right, Robert. I know he can be a bit of an idiot but he's not mad, honestly. It turns out we've all known Sylvene for more or less the same length of time yet none of us know her real name. You see, she made up a different life for each of us. Everything was different... her surname... her work... where she lived..."

"Why did she do that?" said Robert.

Victoria shrugged. "Who knows?"

"I see... and which one do you think is the real Sylvene?"

She shrugged again. "I've no idea."

"It's the first thing I'll ask her when we get back," said Ben, breathing unevenly, his voice shaking with anger.

"You think you will get back?"

Victoria swallowed. "We've got to," she whispered.

"Tell me what you *do* know about her," said Robert seeing her distress.

"There really isn't a lot to tell; Ben met her when she joined his father's archaeological team." Victoria's voice grew stronger. "According to Jonathan she told his family she didn't have to work yet mine understood that she was a courier for one of the larger travel firms..."

"A what?" Robert stared at Victoria.

Victoria giggled again. "Oh dear... I keep forgetting... you won't know about couriers and travel agents. Let me explain..."

"There's no need," Robert said hastily. "It is not important. What I would like to know is what she said to you – when you saw her in the mirror?"

"Who said she said anything?"

Robert grinned, pleased with himself. "Why would she show herself to you if she did not?"

Victoria grinned back. "You're getting too clever!" Her grin vanished as quickly as it had come. The colour faded from her cheeks. "She said we had to find the Sun if we wanted to get home. If we didn't we wouldn't get back. She told me about someone called Gleeman..."

"The Gleeman... why he is..."

"We know who he is – now. At the time we thought it was someone's name. None of us had ever heard of a Gleeman."

Jonathan said: "We found out how wrong we were straight after the wedding ceremony."

"That was a shock." Victoria shivered.

Robert half-smiled. "In my time it is not unusual for travelling musicians to be called a Gleeman."

"Perhaps we should have guessed," Jonathan said slowly. He glanced at his fingers, his eyes troubled. "I know Sylvene warned us to be careful of him but I can't help hoping she's wrong. I like him. He was so proud when the children danced in front of the King. Surely no one who was completely bad would have spent the time he did with them?"

"How often does he come to the village?" Ben said suddenly.

"This is his first visit. The Bailiff met him in Linhest. When he heard about the wedding the Gleeman offered to come and play at it."

"That's not what I heard," said Jonathan. "The

blacksmith told me he used to come to here before the Saxons left."

Robert stiffened. "Conrad said that?"

Clouds scudded across the sky. A plaintive screech broke the uneasy silence. They glanced upwards. Through the gaps in the tree tops they could see a buzzard rolling and turning in the air high above the squat tower of the church. It dived earthward taking them by surprise, wings tight to its body. They held their breath expecting it to crash into the roof. Just as they were about to turn away before it hit the parapet, the buzzard swept upwards on a current of air. For a moment they could see a tiny dot amongst the clouds and then it disappeared.

"Phew!" Jonathan mopped his brow. "That was close…"

"Ssh… Listen…" Robert walked away quickly. As he reached the edge of the copse a twig snapped behind him. He spun round. "Be quiet," he hissed. "It's my father and the Bailiff. Stay here. I'll go and find out what they want."

Jonathan grabbed his arm. "Don't go," he said.

"Why not?" Robert shook himself free. "It's all right, Jonathan. You can trust me," he said very quietly.

"I know we can," said Jonathan, "it's not that… it's the thought of the Bailiff. If he finds out we're here we'll be in real trouble."

Robert tilted his head. The voices were getting fainter. "I don't think you have anything to worry about… I think they're leaving. No, don't move… you make too much noise! Just wait for me here."

He darted away. The others watched him look over the hedge first and then vault the gate easily.

"I don't care what he says," said Ben. "I'm not staying here." He started forward.

Jonathan caught his arm. "We'll wait for him by the hedge," he said.

Taking a deep breath Robert raced across the grass to the church, skidded to a stop, and listened before making his way swiftly along the south wall. Taking care to keep well into the shadows he kept going until he'd reached the front of the church. Stopping, he peeped around the corner.

His father and the Bailiff had already left the churchyard and were heading towards the river. He walked slowly back to the others, his mind still in turmoil.

"Can we come?"

Robert jumped as three heads popped up above the hedge. He smiled uneasily. "Yes, they've gone." He turned away and started back to the church.

Victoria was the first over the gate. But before Jonathan could follow Ben grabbed his arm. "I want to know why you didn't explain about the Rufus Stone?"

He stared, puzzled. "How could I? You-know-what hasn't happened yet?"

"You-know-what… oh…" His eyes widened. "Oh… I didn't think… of course, the King was at the wedding."

"Got it in one," said Jonathan and clambered over the gate.

Laughing, they ran after Robert.

As they approached, he frowned.

"What's wrong?" said Jonathan stopping in front of him.

"I want to believe you," he said. "I really do want to believe you but it is so difficult…"

Her eyes fixed on his face Victoria pulled out the Moon. She held it up. "Would this help?"

Soon all three talismans were spinning at the end of their chains, the gold glinting in the soft sunlight. "Amazing," Robert muttered cupping the Moon in his hands.

"Take them." Jonathan thrust the Star at him. "You can see the rings on the backs."

He examined each in turn before handing them back with a relieved smile. "How can I help?" he asked.

"What made you change your mind?" Victoria's voice wobbled a little as she fastened the chain around her neck.

Ben moved closer to her. Jonathan put his arm around her shoulders. "Yes," he said, "why did you change your mind?"

"I do not know," Robert said with an uneasy laugh. "You tell a strange story. One that is hard to believe…" He looked at Jonathan who didn't flinch under the steady gaze. Robert nodded, his eyes dark and thoughtful. "Yet I trust you."

Ben wiped his face with the sleeve of his tunic.

Jonathan took a step forward, and then hesitated.

Robert smiled at him and at once the tension eased. "Yes I believe you even though what you have told me is difficult to understand... machines that can fly like birds... carts that need no horse..."

"It's all true," Ben said quickly.

Robert chuckled. "I am sure it is; but perhaps it would be wise not to let the Priest hear these tales." His mood changed. "Should he, he would surely order my father to have you burned... as witches."

As Victoria paled he leaned forward and hugged her.

Jonathan glared at him.

Robert grinned slyly: "There is no need to worry," he said. "The Priest will never find out. Now, if we are to find this Sun we should go and search the church."

"You're going to help us?" Ben stared at him.

"Oh yes. But we must be quick. We need to find it before my father sends for me. I was supposed to meet him at the Hall."

Chapter 17
The Sun

"It's no good." Ben stood on the step in front of the altar, his hands on his hips.

Jonathan, Robert and Victoria stopped what they were doing when they heard the anguished cry.

"Why?" said Jonathan, even though he was pretty certain he knew what was wrong.

"The Sun's not here. There's no sign of it anywhere. We must be looking in the wrong place."

"No… I don't believe that." Victoria walked down the nave towards him. "It's got to be here. What else could that cross mean?"

Ben shrugged. His shoulders sagged. He stared at the floor. Away to his right Jonathan gazed unseeingly out of one of the windows. Like the others, he'd been convinced the cross found on the tree meant the church. Now he wasn't so sure. "But we can't just give up," he said half-heartedly.

"Why not?" said Ben. "It all seems rather pointless. We've covered every inch of the building and found nothing. I tell you, Jonathan – it's beginning to feel like some kind of wild goose chase…"

"Wild goose chase?" Robert frowned.

Ben grinned reluctantly. "Forget it Robert – it's just

a stupid saying. What I mean is I don't think that we're going to find the next clue in the church."

"Then why are we searching?" said Robert.

"Don't listen to him," said Jonathan. "Victoria's got the right idea. The clue has to be here."

Ben shook his head. "Oh yeah... so why can't we find it?"

A sudden smile drove away the worried expression on Victoria's face. "We can. It's there." She pointed.

Jonathan blinked. "The altar – impossible. Ben and I checked everything thoroughly."

"I think you'll find you're wrong."

Jonathan frowned. "I'm not. I remember it quite clearly. First we took everything off the altar. When we'd examined that, we put everything back after inspecting... oh." Comprehension dawned.

Victoria chuckled. "You've remembered?"

"Yes. The cross – I was holding the cross when Robert burst into the church, dragging you with him..."

Embarrassed, Robert winced. "Don't remind me. Go on."

"Well before you came in I'd just picked up the cross..."

"We know that," said Ben.

Jonathan glared. "I wish you'd all stop interrupting; where was I – oh yes – I'd picked up the cross as the door flew open." He scratched his head. "That's when things get a bit muddled. The next thing I remember is Victoria telling Robert to put the cross back on the altar."

"And that's what I did," said Robert.

"Yes, you did… but Jonathan think… had you had a proper look at it?

Jonathan shook his head. "I don't think so."

"That's what I'm hoping," Victoria's voice dropped to a whisper. "Jonathan, go and have a look."

He took a step, glanced at Robert and hesitated. "You look."

"Are you sure?"

Jonathan nodded.

"Thank you. I will." Robert ran to the altar paused and bowed, then picked up the cross.

The tension in the church rose as the others watched him intently.

His hand shaking, Robert turned the cross upside down.

"Look at the base. Look at the base." Behind him Victoria was almost jumping up and down with excitement.

Robert grinned at her over his shoulder. "How did you know?"

"It was obvious. Where else could it be?"

Huddled together, they stared at the familiar symbol engraved in the centre of the golden base.

It was Victoria who noticed something unusual. She pointed at the centre ring. "Where's the clue?" she whispered.

"What?" Jonathan grabbed the cross. The light went out of his eyes. "It's not there," he said wearily. "Now what are we going to do?"

A slight smile flickered across Robert's face. He held out his hand. "May I?"

Reluctantly, Jonathan gave him the cross. He turned it upside-down and once again examined the base. "Ahh…" he said softly. "I thought as much. Look at this…"

"What's going on?"

Jonathan, Victoria and Ben spun around.

"Well?" roared the Bailiff. "Answer me – what are you doing here? Why are you not at work?"

"Because I told them to come with me." Robert stepped out from behind the altar, his left hand lightly resting on the hilt of his dagger. He gave Victoria the cross. "Will you put it back?" he said, the smile in his eyes belying his stern expression. "My friends, the Bailiff is right. I should not have kept you from your work." He clapped Jonathan and Ben on their shoulders. "Go while it is still light. Victoria, it is too late for you to go out to the swineherd. My mother will find you some mending to do until the evening meal."

Conrad thrust the iron bar into the glowing coals and signalled to Jonathan to pump the bellows. He watched the growing flames licking the side of the fire box for a moment.

When he was satisfied, he glanced at the figure in the doorway. "Yes, Master Robert?"

Robert smiled and moved closer. "I have come for Jonathan."

The bellows squeaked. The flames died. Conrad frowned at Jonathan who began pumping frantically. As the flames flared again he said: "When do you want him?"

"Now. I am sorry Conrad. I can see you are busy but he is needed back at the Hall."

"Hmm." The blacksmith scowled and pulled the rod from the fire. He laid the red-hot tip across the anvil. "Will he be back in the morning?"

"I think not."

Conrad's eyes darkened. He picked up a heavy hammer. Clang.

The metallic sound rang around the forge as the hammer struck the end of the bar. Sparks flew into the air.

The blacksmith wiped the sweat running down his face with his left arm, grunted and raised the hammer again. "You'm better be off then, lad," he said striking the bar repeatedly.

Robert watched for a moment then added: "I will make sure you get some help in the morning." He turned on his heel and went outside.

To Jonathan's surprise Ben was outside staring at the carvings on the lintel of the porch. Blinking, owl-like in the sudden brightness he shaded his eyes and said: "What's going on?"

Ben shrugged. "I've no idea. Robert turned up at the mill and told me to go with him." He grinned suddenly. "The miller didn't like that."

"What are you two waiting for?" Robert called from the gate to the forge.

"Er… nothing…" Jonathan said. "Where are we going?"

"Back to the compound."

They stared at him.

"The compound… why?" said Ben.

"You'll find out when we get there." Robert looked pleased with himself.

Puzzled, they followed him out of the blacksmith's yard and up the track to the compound. There Robert pointed at a horse and cart standing in front of one of the smaller barns. "That's why you're needed," he said as a man came out of the barn carrying a bundle of hides on one shoulder.

Ben glanced sideways at Jonathan and raised his eyebrows. Jonathan shook his head.

"You are to help load the hides into the cart because in the morning I'm leaving for the market – at Linhest," Robert continued.

Jonathan swallowed. "Isn't this a bit sudden?"

Robert shook his head. "No. My father always sends hides to this market…"

"Master Robert."

He spun round.

Red-faced, his eyes flashing with anger, the Bailiff bustled up to the little group. "Why are they here?" He pointed his whip at Jonathan and Ben, who stepped back out of the reach of the leather thong. "They should be at work."

Robert shot them a warning look. "They are," he said icily. "My father says they are to help load the hides."

Without waiting to hear anything else Jonathan and Ben sidled into the barn. Dust motes floated in a shaft of sunlight streaming through the doorway. The air was heavy with the stench of rotting flesh. Forcing back the rising bile Ben grabbed an armful of hides off a large pile and rushed towards the door and fresh air.

Jonathan followed more slowly, so he didn't see what actually happened. All he knew was one minute Ben was running out of the barn, the next he was sprawling in the dust.

Smiling nastily the Bailiff leaned against the doorframe and pushed him with his foot. "Fool." He raised his whip.

"Be very careful," a quiet voice warned.

The Bailiff stiffened. "Ah… Master Robert. The lad needs to be taught a lesson. He dropped them on purpose."

"I think not. You tripped him… deliberately. No, do not try and deny it. I saw everything."

The man curled his lip. He opened his mouth. Then, as though he'd had second thoughts, closed it and smiled submissively. "An accident Master Robert; a genuine accident." He bent down and began gathering the fallen hides.

Robert watched for a moment before saying: "Good. You can finish loading the cart. Jonathan and Ben come with me."

"Where are we going now?" said Jonathan, uncomfortably aware of the vindictive glare following them.

"To find my father."

"Your father." Ben slowed a little. "Robert, are you really leaving in the morning?"

"Yes, at dawn."

Ben grabbed Jonathan's arm. "In that case – shouldn't we just leave very quietly in the morning as well... before everyone's up?"

Robert frowned.

"There's no need to look like that," Ben said accusingly. "You know what will happen. The minute you drive out of the compound the Bailiff will be on our backs all the time. We'll never be able to search the church again."

"Why would you want to?" said Robert.

Jonathan started, suddenly aware of a hint of laughter in his eyes.

"I'd have thought it was obvious," Ben said. "Or have you forgotten? We've still got to find the Sun."

"Mmm... In that case I can see why you are worried. Maybe this will help." Robert withdrew the dagger from its sheath and pulled out a thin golden chain. He held it out.

"Oh my!" Jonathan stared at the golden Sun. "Where did you find it?"

"Hidden in the cross. There was a tiny bolt on the base which I'd never noticed before. While the Bailiff was shouting at you I opened it and..." Robert beamed, "...there it was..."

Ben drew in his breath. "The Sun!"

"Yes… the Sun."

Ben grinned at him idiotically. "So you found the Sun. Do you realise what that means? Now we can go home."

"It might not be that easy."

Ben jerked round and frowned at Jonathan. "Don't be so gloomy."

"Sorry, I don't want to be a spoilsport but honestly Ben, it isn't that simple."

"Why not?"

"Well, for one thing… we don't know how to find our way back."

"I'd have thought that was obvious. We have to return to the Rufus Stone."

"There is no Rufus Stone… remember?"

"Oh… yes… right… of course I know that... but like it or not the Rufus Stone is where this thing started. I can't believe it'll be that difficult to find Canterton Glen…"

"Canterton Glen?"

"That's the name of the glen, Jonathan. I've been there loads of times with Sylvene and Dad. Once we're back in the forest I'm pretty certain I'll be able to find it. Having said that – it would probably be easier from Lyndhurst."

"Jonathan!" Robert held out the tiny Sun. "You should have this. Take good care of it my friend."

Jonathan stared at the shining sun, finding it difficult to believe he was actually holding the missing talisman. He smiled Robert. "Thank you," he said very softly.

Chapter 18

Linhest

Jonathan woke with a start. Although the Hall was in complete darkness he instinctively knew someone was watching him. He struggled into a sitting position, the hairs on the back of his neck prickling.

"Ssh…" a hand grabbed his shoulder. "It's me, Robert. Don't wake the others. Where's Ben?"

"Next to me, why?"

Robert let go of his shoulder and straightened up. "Wake him and come outside."

By the glowing embers of the fire the Gleeman watched the three shadowy figures leave the Hall. When the door closed on them he turned on his side and shut his eyes.

"Brr… it's cold." Ben shivered and stamped his feet. "Where's Robert?" he grumbled for about the fourth time. "What's he playing at? Why has he left us hanging around here?"

"How should I know?" Jonathan said exasperated by the constant stream of complaints. "All I know was what he said to both of us…that we had to wait here. You heard him. Did he say what for?"

Ben shook his head and tugged at his cloak. Wrapping

it tight around his body he blew on his cold fingers. "Well if he doesn't turn up soon I'm going back to bed. It's too cold…"

"Oh do shut up – it's boring."

"Don't tell me to…"

Jonathan nudged him. "Forget it… Look, here he comes."

Ben peered into a darkness that was now streaked with light stealing in from the east. He scowled. "Who's that with him? Is it Victoria?"

"My son, is everything ready?"

Startled, they spun round. Sir Henry was standing in the doorway of the barn where the hides had been. Robert ran to him and bowed.

Victoria dashed across to Jonathan and Ben. "Is it true?" she whispered.

"Is what true?"

"That Robert found the Sun?"

Jonathan nodded. "Believe it or not it *was* in the cross."

"Thought so…" she glanced around, puzzled. "What's happening? Why are we here?"

"You tell us." Ben scowled darkly.

Jonathan glared at him, then smiled at Victoria. "I think Robert's getting ready to leave."

"What if he is? Did he need to get us up to see him off?" Ben said sullenly.

As though he'd overheard Jonathan, Robert clambered on to the driver's seat, gathered up the reins and said to the groom holding the horse's head: "You can let go now. Father, are the hides fastened securely?"

"Yes my son."

"Good. And is the piece of bacon and sack of flour my mother is sending to her sister safely stowed on board as well?"

Sir Henry checked the back of the cart. "They are Robert, as is the crate of chickens for your aunt. Be sure to give our gifts to Lady Thorp as soon as you reach Linhest. Here boy," he handed Jonathan a bow and quiver full of arrows. "Stow these under the driver's seat."

"Robert... Robert..." Lady Faversham's cheerful voice rang around the compound.

"Yes mother?" Robert smiled as she bustled up, clutching a wicker basket.

She held it up. "T'is one of my cheeses. Can you find room for it? Pray say you can. My sister always enjoys my cheese."

"Of course, mother. Put it in the cart. Father, we must go if we are to reach Linhest before nightfall. Ben, Victoria, each of you find a place to sit in the back of the cart, Jonathan you are to come up here."

"What?" They stared at Robert.

He chuckled. "Why so surprised? Didn't I say? You are to accompany me to Linhest."

"Linhest... isn't that..."

"In the Forest... yes Jonathan. My father agrees – it is time for you to leave our house and continue your journey to London. When the winter sets in the roads across the forest can become quite impassable. I believe you will find it easier to start from Linhest. Isn't that right, Ben?"

Ben stared at him, stunned into silence.

Robert grew more serious. "We must go. Take your place, Jonathan. Ben, Victoria, are you ready?"

"We're ready," Victoria called.

"Good." Robert leaned over the side of cart and held out his hand. "Father, you have the permit?"

"Here my son." Sir Henry placed a leather pouch in his hand. "Take great care of it. Mind you keep to the main track. Remember the King is hunting in the forest."

Robert nodded.

Sir Henry raised his arm. "Go then and God speed."

"I can't believe we're actually leaving," Victoria sounded almost sad as the cart trundled through the village.

Once clear of the huts Robert turned the horse towards the bridge. Rain began to fall. A gentle, persistent rain; but by the time the large, open fields had been left behind the clouds had moved away and the sun was beginning to shine.

In the forest the only sign of rain were the tiny glistening droplets of water caught in the thick gorse brakes and bracken fronds lining the track.

Jonathan, Victoria and Ben peered around, each secretly hoping to see something familiar. Something that would show they were on the right track. Jonathan began chatting to Robert. In the back of the cart Ben and Victoria drowsed, lulled by the heat of the sun and the gentle swaying.

They drove past groups of ponies that stopped grazing and turned their heads towards them. Ears pricked they would watch the cart for a moment before wheeling around and galloping away.

With Robert whistling softly they passed through woodlands of beech and oak; over barren heathland; around the occasional peat bog. But when the sun began to sink towards the horizon the whistling died away and Robert became increasingly anxious. If the horse slowed he would flick the thong of his whip along its back until it increased its pace. His hands gripped the reins so tightly the knuckles turned white.

At last Jonathan nudged him. "What's wrong? Why the hurry?"

Robert grimaced. "The town's gates close at sunset. If we're too late we will have to spend the night in the forest."

"What's that?" Ben jerked out of his stupor. He prodded Victoria. "Robert reckons we might have to camp in the forest if we don't reach Lyndhurst before sunset."

Jonathan frowned. "I don't think there's any need to worry. We'll either get there in time or we won't. Whatever happens we won't be alone. Look over there…" he pointed at a line of travellers making for the horizon…"if we don't get to the town in time, neither will they."

Victoria yawned, sat up and looked around curiously. They were overtaking a man and woman driving a small flock of sheep along the side of the track. Hearing a faint tune borne on the breeze, reminded her of something else. "I wonder if the Gleeman has noticed we've gone yet," she said dreamily.

"He might have. He certainly will when we don't turn up for supper tonight," said Jonathan. "The question is – will he come after us?"

"Do you think he's the person Sylvene warned us about?"

"Of course." Jonathan grimaced. Deep down he didn't know what to think. He liked the man. Yet if what Sylvene had said was true…

"Look – Linhest." Robert half-stood and pointed at a spiral of smoke they could see rising above the horizon. He tapped the horse. Snorting it shook its head and broke into a lumbering canter, the cart creaking ominously.

As they approached the town the traffic grew heavier and Robert was forced to slow the pace again.

He was weaving the cart between a man leading a couple of heifers and a group of richly clad merchants on fine horses when he suddenly pulled up. Leaning over the side of the cart he said: "Father, would you like a ride?"

The monk – his face streaked with grime, his bare feet covered in dust – smiled back. "Bless you my son." Hitching his robes above his knees he climbed on board and slipped into the small space Ben and Victoria had managed to make.

Robert cracked the whip and the horse set off again. Breathing heavily, the monk scratched his ear then wiped his nose on the back of his hand. "This is most welcome," he said, leaning against a bundle of the hides. "My feet are sore. I have been on the road for many days."

"Do you think we will reach the safety of the town before the gates close?" Robert said.

"We will, have no fear." The monk wriggled forward and kneeled behind the driver's seat. The cart lurched and tilted as it rolled over a badly rutted length of the track. He caught hold of one of the sides and held on tight. "Although it is near sundown there is not much farther to go. Trust me my son. We will reach Linhest in time."

And they did.

As the horse walked slowly though the gateway past the sentries the monk leaned forward and tapped Robert on the shoulder. "I will leave you here." He jumped over the side of the moving cart and looked up. "God bless you my son," he said making the sign of the cross.

"How much farther do we have to go?" asked Jonathan watching their unusual companion disappear into an alley.

"Not far." Robert flicked the reins.

The cart swung into a narrow side street. At once the sun vanished, hidden by protruding floors of the houses on either side of the street that almost touched each other across the cobbles.

Robert pulled the horse up in front of a large two-storied house built mainly of brick, the square windows filled with expensive glass. He handed Jonathan the reins. "Hold these," he said and climbed down.

Grasping the heavy knocker on the front door he rapped loudly. The door creaked and swung outward. Silhouetted in the opening was a slight man, his hair grey and thinning. He bowed. "Welcome Master Robert. My Lord Thorp is in the library."

"Thank you, Joseph. Will you see to the horse?"

"Of course, Master Robert." Joseph bowed again and went to the animal's head.

Robert turned and beckoned. "Come – we will go and find my Uncle."

Jonathan, Victoria and Ben followed him into the imposing candle-lit hall and stopped in front of a wide wooden staircase winding its way up to the upper floor. Next to it was a huge fireplace. Robert pointed at a heavy oak door at the far end of the hall.

"That's the library."

He crossed the floor, knocked and opened the door. The others crowded behind him. They could see that three of the walls were lined with oak panels; the fourth wall was hidden behind rows of shelves. By the casement was a small round table, with two chairs on opposite sides. The occupant of the room, an elderly man, was leaning against a high stone mantle staring into a blazing log fire.

He looked up and stepped forward, his arms

outstretched. "My boy." He embraced Robert. "You are very welcome." A movement behind his nephew caught his eye. "Who have we here?"

"Travellers, Uncle Thorp. They have been helping my family with the harvest and are now on their way to London to seek work. My mother thought you would not mind me bringing them here."

Lord Thorp shook his head. "Of course not, they are most welcome."

Robert smiled. "Thank you. They have worked hard for us and my family has become fond…"

"Enough Robert. Any friend of your family will always be welcome in my house." He beckoned. "Come in. Come in. When my Lady returns, she will organise sleeping quarters for all of you."

Chapter 19
Market Day

Lady Thorp pushed back her chair and stood. "Husband, Victoria is exhausted. I will show her to her bedchamber. Pray, do not keep the young men up longer than necessary. They must also be tired. Remember, Robert is to rise early in the morning to meet the leather merchant."

It had been a delicious meal. By far the best since they'd arrived in Norman England. Roast venison with masses of fresh vegetables; an herbal salad; loaves of warm, newly baked bread; a selection of cheeses and the first of this year's apple crop.

The greatest surprise had been the knives and spoons. Jonathan, Victoria and Ben couldn't believe it when they saw them on the table. That, and the fact that the food had been served on pewter plates instead of trenchers, had made the meal even more enjoyable.

Lord Thorp smiled tranquilly at his elegant wife. "Very well, my dear. But first I want to give Robert the news from London. Your Aunt Montfort, my dear boy, has been safely delivered of a fine son."

"That is indeed good news…"

"Come child." Lady Thorp guided Victoria from the dining room into the hall. She led her up the wide curving staircase and along the landing. Stopping by a door she lifted the latch and smiled at Victoria. "This is where you will sleep. I hope the noise will not disturb you," she added in her gentle way, crossing the floor to close a window that overlooked the front street as a shout of raucous laughter rang out.

"I don't think that would be possible." Victoria yawned. Still yawning she glanced around at her surroundings. The room was light and airy. Intricate tapestries covered the walls.

Rugs not rushes covered the floor. Best of all was the bed.

She hugged herself. It was all so different from the communal sleeping quarters she had had to share with the other single women of East Oakhurst. There she had two threadbare and smelly skins covering a heap of straw in a dark and squalid hut.

Tonight she would sleep in a handsome wooden bed made up with fresh linen, alone, and in a large and airy room.

At East Oakhurst there had been no fresh water to wash in except that drawn from a nearby stream. The sun and wind had been her towels.

Here there was a basin of water on top of a stand in the corner of the room. On the shelf below she could see a pile of crisp, white cloths.

Never mind the noise – this was perfection.

Lady Thorp touched her arm and smiled. "I will bid you goodnight, child," she said and left the room, closing the door quietly.

Almost before the door had closed Victoria lay

down and pulled the bed linen up to her chin. Almost immediately she began twisting and turning in an attempt to get comfortable; but whatever she did the mattress remained hard and unyielding. She sat up and pinched it. Probably horse-hair she thought peering under the bed. As she'd expected there weren't any springs. No wonder it was so uncomfortable. Still, with a bit of luck nothing would keep her awake tonight, she decided lying down again.

Outside the locked gates the travellers who had arrived too late to enter the town huddled in little groups around brightly burning fires. As the night drew on a few wrapped themselves in their cloaks and, curled up on the ground, slept. Most stayed awake, talking and keeping an anxious eye on their goods. Only the sound of dogs howling, or the soft melodious notes of a flute carried on the breeze, broke the monotony of the night.

In the town householders, both rich and poor, closed the shutters of their homes and retired to bed for the night. The market vendors who had arrived in good time covered their goods and slept under their stalls.

A shaft of sunlight streamed in through the window and fell across Robert's face. He sat up, stretched then slipped from the bed. Outside the window he could hear voices. Pulling on his shoes he ran from the room and down the stairs just as Joseph walked through the hall carrying a bundle of logs.

"Wait Joseph," he called.

Joseph turned his head. "Good morning Master Robert."

"My Uncle – is he up?"

"Lord Thorp is in the stables showing Peter Jenkins the hides you brought."

"Ah… so the leather merchant has arrived. Thank you." Robert ran to the side door and paused. "Oh, and Joseph..."

"Yes Master Robert?"

"When my friends come down – tell them to wait for me in the hall." He pushed open the door and went outside.

"Ah, there you are. My boy, come and meet Peter Jenkins." Lord Thorp clapped a hand on Robert's shoulder and whispered in his ear: "He seems very interested in the hides. I think he might well buy them." Straightening up he boomed: "Peter, this is my nephew – the one who brought these excellent skins."

The round apple of a man bending over the back of the cart stood up and bowed, his leather jerkin creaking under the strain. Robert grinned. But his smile faded when he saw the merchant studying him with an expression both shrewd and knowing. Aware that he would be unable to compete he returned the bow and edged behind his uncle in the hope he would continue to conduct the haggling.

Jonathan turned on his back, stared at the ceiling and

yawned. It had felt quite strange, sleeping in a bed again. If he was honest he hadn't slept that well. Once he'd almost got out to lie on the floor. But he hadn't and eventually he'd fallen asleep.

He sat up, wishing for the hundredth time that he still had his wristwatch. He pushed back the bedclothes and went to the window. Behind him, Ben rolled into the space he'd left. Jonathan opened the shutters and leaned out. It must still be quite early. The sun was only just peeping above the roof-tops. He glanced down into the yard.

Robert was sitting on an upturned barrel directly beneath his window. Lord Thorp was talking to a stranger who was examining the hides.

The leather merchant... Jonathan thought remembering what Lady Thorp had said just before taking Victoria up to bed after dinner. As though aware he was being watched Robert glanced up, grinned and beckoned.

Jonathan mouthed: "In a moment," and went back to the bed. He prodded Ben in the ribs. "Wake up."

"Whad... why... I don't want to." Ben dragged a rug over his head.

Jonathan sat on the edge of the mattress and pulled on his shoes. "You've got to. Robert's already up. Come on. Let's go and find Victoria."

"Why?"

"Because he wants us down in the courtyard."

"Who does?"

"For goodness sakes haven't you listened to anything I've said... Robert? Why all the questions?"

Throwing off the rug, Ben sat up and glared at him. "Why all the questions? Because I don't want to get out of bed – that's why."

"Well you've got to… so get a move on."

Jonathan and Victoria dashed down the stairs. Ben lagged behind.

"Good news!" Robert called entering the hall. "The merchant has bought the hides."

Victoria clapped her hands. "Jonathan said he thought you'd sold them. Can we leave now?"

Robert laughed and shook his head. "No. My Aunt has gone to the market – to find some material for Mother. And I have a list of things to buy. We will stay one more night and leave early in the morning."

Victoria swallowed and turned her head away.

Jonathan put his arm around her. "Come on… we've been here so long what's one more night? Let's have a look at the market… it might be fun."

Victoria smiled and dashed away some unfallen tears. "Sorry, I'm being stupid… I know."

Robert smiled. "That would be good. If you wait here I will fetch my list." He started up the stairs taking them two at a time.

Jonathan could feel the excitement in the air even before the front door closed, shutting them out of the house. It was hard to believe that ahead stretched a whole day – a day in which they could do as much or as little as they wanted without being told off or ordered elsewhere.

Laughing cheerfully they hurried down the street taking care to avoid the open drain running along the centre. At the far end they tagged on to the tail of the good-natured crowd pushing its way into the market place.

Once there, they stared amazed at the assortment of stalls that had been crammed into every available space. There were stalls of different sizes and shapes; stalls open to the elements, stalls with fancy awnings protecting the vendors from both sun and rain. A few were simple wooden tables, others merely a collection of boxes.

A huge variety of goods was offered for sale; eggs and cheeses; vegetables; crates of live chickens or pigeons stacked one on top of another. There were the luxuries coveted by wealthy merchants and their wives… fine muslins, silks, linens and wool; hose, shoes and sandals; beautiful intricate jewellery fashioned by craftsmen.

Some stallholders sold weapons; bows and arrows, hunting daggers, swords and shields. Nearby were the saddlers with their bridles, saddles and harnesses.

Jonathan picked up a horse collar, grimaced and dropped it again. "Phew… pity the poor horse…"

"Move boy." A large hand dragged him out of the way of a well-dressed man being ushered towards an ornate saddle by the fawning stallholder.

Chuckling at the sudden flash of anger in Jonathan's eyes, Robert led them along the line of stalls, stopping occasional to consult his lists.

It was like market day at home – except for the haggling – Jonathan thought, waiting with Ben and Victoria while Robert completed yet another purchase. He glanced sideways. Two men were comparing prices and craftsmanship, their expressions deliberately blank.

A pungent scent filled the air.

Robert tilted his head and breathed deeply. "Spices!" He ran his finger down his mother's list. "I thought so. Come on."

"Where's he going now?" Ben grumbled squeezing past a richly dressed couple engrossed in choosing a brooch.

"To find the spices I guess," said Jonathan, fighting his way through another mass of people. For a moment it seemed as though they might have lost Robert in the middle of the swirling throng. But when the numbers thinned again they saw him, some distance away, crossing the road.

They hurried towards him as a troupe of acrobats and tumblers rushed by – like a giant wave – scattering everyone in their path. Faces flashed around them. The acrobats somersaulted onto a raised wooden platform set in front of the town's church.

The crowd pressed forward. Keeping close to the platform and holding aloft bunches of brightly coloured ribbons the tumblers raced round and round, creating a giant circle out of the audience. Laughter swelled and bubbled while the acrobats somersaulted and cart-wheeled around the platform. Cheering loudly the spectators threw handfuls of coins on to the stage. In a final frenzy the acrobats twisted and turned into impossible shapes then flung themselves into the air. Landing in a line they knelt on one knee and doffed their caps.

A sudden roar from further down the street drowned out the cheers of the watching crowd. Jonathan shook Ben's arm. "Stay with Victoria," he said turning. He pushed his way through the watching people and ran down the road to join the back of this second, laughing crowd.

"Eh, lad." A heavy hand caught him between the shoulder blades. "'Tis a goodly show. You don't want to miss it."

Grateful, Jonathan slid into the gap the man made for him and peered over the head immediately in front. His stomach heaved. He turned away oblivious to his surroundings.

"Watch it boy," a rough voice protested when he stood on its owner's foot.

"Sorry," he whispered hoarsely. He swallowed. "I've got to go… my friends are waiting." Around him people grumbled good-naturedly as he pushed past blindly, trying to block out the memory of the pathetic figure dancing its tormented dance.

"Let's go," he said, reaching Victoria and Ben at last.

"Why?" Victoria said. "I'm not in a hurry. This is fun. What's happening down there? Is it worth going to see?"

Jonathan bit his lip. "Bear baiting. They're bear baiting."

Victoria gasped. She looked around. Robert was watching the jugglers. She pushed past Jonathan and grabbed his hand. "What can we do?" she cried.

"Do?" He stared at her. "I do not understand. What is it you want to do?"

"Stop the bear-baiting of course. It's cruel."

"Oh that!" Robert laughed. "'Tis only a bit of fun."

Jonathan glanced at Victoria. There was a determined glint in her eye – a glint he'd come to know only too well. He leaned closer and whispered: "It is horrible, I know. But try and remember where we are – it's the Middle Ages. You mustn't blame Robert."

Victoria's eyes widened. Instead of the angry retort he'd expected she pointed a shaking finger. A figure was standing at the back of the platform. "How did he get here so quickly?" she whispered.

Chapter 20
The Gleeman

Streams of ribbons, vibrant reds, blues and greens, swirled above the crowd. Dancers joined the group. But neither Jonathan nor Ben noticed. Their attention, like Victoria's, was fixed on the figure at the back of the platform tapping his foot in time to the music he was playing.

The Gleeman!

The tempo increased. The dancers twisted and turned, spun and swayed, their feet barely touching the ground. But despite their expertise it was the tumblers and acrobats who were the real focus of the people. Their human pyramids and complicated backward flips kept the audience gasping with delightful fear.

Five men at the bottom of a pyramid, their arms intertwined and hands on their neighbour's shoulders, staggered slightly every time another member of the troupe leapt into the air and landed on the topmost row. At last only one more man was needed to finish the pyramid. A drum beat out a sharp tattoo. The tension increased when a slender figure darted out from behind the Gleeman and cart-wheeled across the stage. The audience caught its breath.

With a flip the lad somersaulted through the air. A sharp hiss reverberated around the platform. The boy landed on the shoulders of the top two men. A roar rang out. Cymbals crashed. The pyramid swayed dangerously. The audience froze and gasped. The tower of men steadied. Loud cheers erupted again. Men threw their caps in the air. All around the audience stamped their feet with approval.

One by one the tumblers and dancers dropped to one knee half-turned and raised an arm in a triumphant gesture at the stage. One by one the acrobats in the pyramid somersaulted into the air and landed on the platform in a semi-circle. When all were safely down they linked hands, stepped forward and bowed.

The audience roared their appreciation. Waving, the acrobats slipped away. Now, each holding a sequinned cap, several small children stormed into the crowd to catch the coins being flung in every direction.

While the rest of the musicians joined the troupe the Gleeman jumped down from the front of the platform. Robert stepped forward and held out his hand. Jonathan, Ben and Victoria remained were they were, watching him warily.

The Gleeman smiled, a thoughtful deliberate smile and grasped the hand. "We meet again, Master Robert."

"We do indeed. I trust you left my family in good spirits."

"I did and in excellent health. I was saddened to leave the village. Your family had made me most welcome. But the time had come for me to follow my destiny."

"It didn't take you long to get here." Victoria glared

defiantly at him from the safety of Jonathan's side.

"True, young Mistress. I was fortunate. On the way here I met with friends – the troupe of acrobats you have just had the good fortune to watch. Together we travelled through the forest, not stopping… even at night. T'was as though they had wings on their feet."

"You said you were going to follow your destiny. Where do you want your destiny to take you?" asked Jonathan.

The Gleeman shrugged. "Who knows, young Master. But you may be very sure I go where I am needed. Perhaps we will meet again… in the future."

Victoria shivered. "Not if I see you first," she whispered.

The Gleeman doffed his cap. He bowed. "I have tarried too long. I fear I must join my companions," he said. When he straightened up there was no smile on his face. Instead, he turned on his heel and left.

"Do you think he's following us?" Victoria said watching the dancers surround him.

"Possibly." Jonathan turned to Robert. "What do you think? Did he follow us here?"

Robert raised an eyebrow. "Follow you? Why would he want to do that?"

"Because… oh I don't know. I like him, but he says so many confusing things. Sometimes I think he knows we're strangers in the twelfth century. Other times I'm not so sure. And then there was Sylvene's warning…"

"My friend, the man is doing what his kind always

does – travelling from town to town, playing his flute to make an honest living. Forget about him. There are more important things for you to worry about – like finding this Canterton Glen that Ben spoke about before we left East Oakhurst.

"But first we must buy some more things. Only when that is done can we make our plans for the journey. Victoria, my mother needs a new comb. Will you help me choose it?"

The rest of the afternoon was spent walking up and down the market searching for furs for the coming winter, salt for preserving meat, herbs and spices to make the salted meat more palatable. There were the silks and needles Robert's mother wanted, cooking utensils for the cook, a hunting knife for Sir Henry. When the final item on the list – a large black cooking pot – had been purchased Robert rubbed his hands together. "Good! Now we can return to my aunt's house."

"Thank goodness for that," Victoria said with feeling. "I think if I don't sit down soon I'll fall down. My feet are killing me."

Robert reached for the hilt of his dagger, his eyes flashing. "Where is the villain?"

"What 'villain'?" Victoria looked at him, puzzled.

"The one that is killing you."

Jonathan, Ben and Victoria burst out laughing.

Robert stared at them.

"Relax, put it away Robert," Jonathan said suppressing his laughter with difficulty. "Nobody's killing Victoria.

It's a saying from our time. My feet are killing me means '*my feet are hurting*'. That's why she wants to sit down."

Robert thrust the knife into its sheath. He shook his head. "Strange… quite strange these time walkers," he muttered moving off again.

Sleep was a long time coming that night for Jonathan. Each time it began to steal over him the thin face of the Gleeman, his startling blue eyes intense and stern, swam into view and he would wake with a start. When he did finally fall asleep his dreams were disturbed by dark images – dancing bears playing flutes; men and women their faces hidden behind raven masks dragging a screaming Victoria from his grasp; the Gleeman walking across to talk to a woman standing on the other side of the street watching and laughing.

Jonathan woke with a start, beads of perspiration on his forehead. What was Sylvene doing in his dream? And why did the Gleeman want to speak to her? He rubbed his eyes, wearily. What on earth did the dream mean?

"Ben," he put out his hand and frowned. The space beside him was empty. Jonathan sat up and looked around the room. Ben was sitting, cross-legged, on the window seat staring out at the cool, slate-grey sky heavily stained with fierce, flaming streaks.

"What are you doing?"

"Nothing – I'm just thinking."

"Thinking what?"

Ben shook his head. "It doesn't matter. Do you want to see something funny? Robert's trying to back the horse into the shafts of the cart... Oops he's missed again. Hey, where are you going?" he said as Jonathan shot out of bed

"To help him of course." Jonathan stopped at the door and looked back. "Why didn't you wake me?"

Ben shrugged.

Jonathan shook his head. "Well, aren't you coming?" he said, losing patience.

"No... I told you... I'm thinking."

Jonathan glared at him. Even though they'd only known each other for a comparatively short time he knew that when Ben was in this sort of mood there was no point in arguing. He walked along the landing and knocked on Victoria's door.

"Who is it?" she called sleepily.

"Jonathan."

The door opened a crack and she peered out. "You're up early."

"Not as early as Robert. He's already in the yard loading the cart."

Victoria smiled and her face lit up. "Great! He said we'd be leaving today."

"I'm going to help. Do you want to come?"

"Try and stop me. Wait a moment while I get my shoes."

At the bottom the stairs Victoria caught hold of Jonathan's arm. "It's not a dream, is it? We really are going home – aren't we?"

He smiled and pulled her close. "Yes, we really are," he whispered in her ear hugging her tight. With his arm around her shoulder he led her outside, letting the door slam behind them.

Hearing the loud thud Robert turned. Two figures, one slight, the other tall and skinny, were walking towards him. He finished fastening the throat lash of the bridle and waited.

"Is everything on?" Jonathan called.

He shook his head. "There's still the bale of linen and some cooking utensils as well as the herbs and spices..." He held out the reins. "Victoria, would you hold these while Jonathan and I get the rest of the things?"

She backed away. "Er... I'm not sure..."

Robert laughed: "Go on. Take it. He won't hurt you."

The horse snorted and tossed his head.

"Er... are you sure about that?"

Robert grinned. "Quite sure. He's much too quiet. Just talk to him if he gets fidgety." He frowned and looked around. "Where's Ben?"

Victoria stopped gazing at her reflection in the horse's dark and soulful eyes and glanced up at a window.

Robert followed her gaze. "I see. Well, if he's not down by the time we're ready to leave I'll go and get him myself."

Victoria giggled.

Chapter 21

Hunting Again

"My boy." Lord Thorp grasped the horse by its mane and fixed his eyes on Robert who was now sitting on the driver's box. "Are you ready to leave?"

"Yes sir... apart from Ben."

"Hmm... where is the lad?"

Robert glanced up at the window and frowned. "I wish I knew. He was up there earlier, up but he seems to have gone... no, wait... isn't that him?" He pointed at a figure leaning against the wall of the stable, watching them.

Sir Henry squinted. "It's difficult to see." He raised his voice. "Over here boy – Robert is ready to leave and you're companions are anxious to start for London."

Embarrassed, Ben shot across the courtyard.

From the back of the cart Jonathan glared at him. "What have you been doing? We've been hanging around here waiting for you for ages."

"That's a bit of an exaggeration." Victoria wriggled further down amongst the parcels then leaned against the black cooking pot. "That's better. Now tell the truth Jonathan – we've actually only just got into the cart."

Jonathan grinned sheepishly.

"What's this? What's this? I understood your friends were to go to London?" Puzzled, Lord Thorp stared at

Ben who had swung himself on to the box and was now sitting next to Robert. "Their way is not your way. They should leave Linhest through the east gate."

Robert tensed. "I know my Lord."

"Then why are they in the cart?"

Robert reddened. "Uncle my friends do not know the way to the east gate. I said I would take them there before going home."

"Madness Robert... it will delay your journey considerably." Lord Thorp stepped back from the horse. He gazed at his scowling nephew and shook his head. "Oh, very well... if you insist... take them. But first you must promise me that you will stay on the track when you drive across the forest."

Robert nodded.

"Good. The King's hunting party left here at dawn. It would be dangerous to stray from your way. Enough now... if you are to reach East Oakhurst before darkness falls you should leave immediately. Remember me to your mother and father. Thank them for all the good things you brought with you to our humble home."

Robert smiled, transforming his face. He gathered up the reins. "I will, uncle. And thank you for everything you have done for us." He cracked the whip, skimming the tip over the horse's back. Snorting, it tossed its head. He flicked the reins. The horse strained against the harness. Slowly and with a loud creaking the wheels of the cart began to turn.

"Phew, well done Robert – that was quick thinking,"

said Jonathan staring back at Lord Thorp who was standing, motionless by the stables, one hand raised in farewell.

Robert steered the horse and cart through the archway and out to the street. "I do not like to deceive my elders," he said when he had successfully finished a particularly tricky manoeuvre through the crowds streaming along the road in the opposite direction, "but sometimes I fear 'tis necessary."

The wheels rattled over the cobbles as Robert navigated a way through the narrow streets lined on either side by rows of sturdy houses. At one junction he had to turn the horse to the left and under an archway. At the next bend he half-stood and pointed with his whip. "There it is – the west gateway."

The horse slowed to a walk. Robert glanced over his shoulder. "Don't say a word," he ordered quietly. "If anyone asks a question just leave the talking to me."

But the two sentries on duty merely yawned as the cart approached and waved it through. Ahead stretched the track and familiar landscape they'd driven across a couple of days earlier. The only difference was that today, instead of a steady stream of people in holiday mood making for the town and market, the road was empty.

Larks sang as they drove past the thick, purple heather on either side of the track, crickets chirruped. Even so Jonathan felt uneasy. The peace was deceptive he thought looking around. Uncertainty and danger lay ahead.

It must have been nearly noon when Robert drove the cart off the track and pulled up the horse under a huge oak tree. A faint frown creased his forehead.

The others glanced at each other.

"Is there a problem?" asked Jonathan at last.

"A small one. I need to ask Ben something." He turned to him, "do you see that bend ahead?"

Ben nodded.

"Well, beyond that there is a fork in the road. What I need to know is – which track do we take?"

Ben rubbed the back of his neck. He shook his head his eyes dark and troubled. "I'm sorry… it's hopeless. I simply don't know."

"Ben!" Victoria sat up with a start.

Ben refused to meet her eyes. "Don't look like that. I can't help it. Ever since we got to Lyndhurst I've been trying to remember the way to the glen. That's why I didn't come down to help this morning. And I sat up most of last night…"

"But Ben, you were so sure. You more or less promised that once we were there you'd know the way back," Victoria cried.

"I'm sorry," Ben said his eyes still troubled. "I thought it would be easy… but the forest is so different to the one we've left behind. Honestly, I can't tell you how sorry I am. I've let you all down." He bit his lip. "I've made a mess of everything."

They stared at him.

"I'm so sorry," he said again.

"It's not your fault," Jonathan said quickly. "Don't worry. I'm sure we can work it out."

"Of course we can. If it's any help, I think we should take the left hand track."

The three boys turned to Victoria.

Ben bit his right thumbnail. "How could you possibly know?"

"I did what Jonathan said – worked it out! The right fork would take us back to East Oakhurst – wouldn't it Robert?"

"Yes."

"Ben, you said the glen was west of Lyndhurst. Are you sure that's correct?"

He nodded.

"Then think about it. We don't want to go to East Oakhurst we want to go westward. So we have to take the left hand fork."

Ben grinned with relief. His shoulders sagged. "You know, she's right. Robert, we have to take… what is it Jonathan?" he said seeing the expression on his face.

Jonathan raised his hand. "Listen."

They sat, transfixed, each straining their ears while the horse pulled at a clump of grass. Suddenly he stopped eating and lifted his head, his ears pricked. High and clear the distinctive call of a hunting horn could be heard floating across the forest. A horse whinnied. Dogs yelped excitedly.

"'Tis the King's hunting party." Robert gave an uneasy laugh. "Remember what my uncle said – the King is hunting in the forest today. This changes everything. We cannot leave the track. We have to take the way to East Oakhurst. It would be too dangerous to do otherwise."

The horn sounded again, this time louder and accompanied by the thud of hooves flying over hard, sun-scorched earth and the baying of hounds in full cry. With a high, terrified whinny their horse shied, careered on to the track and bolted.

Robert grabbed at the reins dangling dangerously near to the wheels. Half-standing, he sawed at the bit. The cart swayed crazily over the potholes and ruts scarring the track. Afraid he might be thrown off at any moment Ben clung desperately to the driver's seat. Behind him Jonathan and Victoria clutched the wooden sides. For a few terrifying minutes the horse kept up the panic-stricken gallop. The knuckles on Robert's hands were white with the strain but, very gradually, he got the horse back under control.

When he was sure it wouldn't bolt again he sank down beside Ben and pointed, his hand shaking. "Look – over there."

"The King," Jonathan breathed staring at the richly dressed man astride a gleaming grey horse deep in conversation with a group of riders by the edge of a copse.

"And over there," said Robert swinging his hand to their left. Downwind, a dozen or so foot-followers were encouraging hounds to cast around for a scent.

Jonathan's skin prickled and he gave a low whistle. "We've been seen," he warned the others.

"What do we do now?" Ben said, his voice tight and anxious as he stared at the huntsman watching them.

"What do you think, Robert?" said Victoria.

Robert wiped his sweaty hands on his tunic. "Just keep going. If we do not stray from the track we are safe."

"Doesn't that mean we'll end up back at East Oakhurst?" Jonathan said.

Robert laughed. "Trust me my friend. That will not happen. But I have no wish to be hauled in front of the King – even if he has had a good day in the forest – for that is what would happen should we be caught away from our permitted route. When we have left the hunt behind we will look for your mysterious glen."

"They're moving off again," Jonathan said, watching the hunt.

"Which way?" Robert asked quickly.

"Southwards," said Jonathan.

Gradually the yelping of hounds was replaced by the sounds of the forest. Robert laughed with relief. "We are safe now," he said as the track took them into a wood away from the danger of the hunting party.

The light was dim except for the occasional drop of sunlight falling through the tangle of leaves on to the path. The horse walked on steadily, the cart bouncing over the roots protruding from the track. Once, they caught a glimpse of a deer crashing through the undergrowth.

As Robert urged the horse on Victoria looked around, her eyes wide and anxious. Catching sight of her pale face, Jonathan squeezed her hand.

She relaxed a little and smiled. "I'm all right, thanks. It's just… look… isn't that blue sky I can see ahead? We must be coming out… no… wait… Robert… over there… behind that holly bush."

Robert pulled up the horse.

"It's another track," Jonathan said, his eyes narrowing.

Robert turned the horse. Almost immediately the path began to climb, gradually at first, then much steeper. On and on they went up the side of the hill. Victoria leaning against Jonathan, watched the changing landscape. They were nearly at the top of the hill when she sat up with a jolt.

Jonathan watched, amused at her sudden change of expression. A smile twitched at the corners of his lips – but vanished when she started to stand.

"Here… hang on… you'll fall out if you're not careful…" he shouted as the front wheel hit the edge of a pothole.

Victoria clutched at him, missed and fell on to the handle of the iron pot. "Ouch… that hurt." She rubbed her hip. "There's no need to look so smug. I bet you don't know where we are?"

"Well… no."

"I do."

A light breeze rustled the leaves. Something in a clump of bracken beside the path screeched loudly. Jonathan jumped. "Probably a pheasant," he muttered, embarrassed.

Victoria nodded. "Probably… but there's something

else. Something you've missed. Just listen… oh, come on… you must be able to hear it."

Jonathan tilted his head. What was it he was missing? He held his breath. He grinned. Leaning over the side of the cart he peered through a gap in the trees, straightened up and looked at Victoria. "Water. I can hear water. There's a stream at the bottom of the gully."

She smiled. "Now do you recognize where we are?"

He shook his head. "No. Should I?"

She nodded. "Remember what I said? I think I know where we are."

Jonathan stared at her.

Victoria sighed. "Do I have to spell it out? It's important to remember that this is my first visit to the Forest. So if I can recognize this place it must mean only one thing… I've been here this holiday."

Oh!" His face cleared. "I see what you're saying. This is the way we came when we left the Rufus Stone?"

"Yes. It has to be." Victoria's eyes sparkled.

"…and at the top of this hill is the ridge where we saw the hunt." Excitement crept into Jonathan's voice.

Laughing, Victoria grabbed his arm as the cart emerged from the trees into the sunshine. "Look, I was right. Down there is where we saw the hunt and…"

"What are you two going on about?" Ben said turning around in his seat.

"This is where we saw the hunt." Victoria cried. "Don't you remember? The deer broke cover from that thicket, jumped over that fallen tree and took off across the heathland…"

"Remember?" Ben shook his head. "Aren't you forgetting something? I wasn't with you. I was tied up in the back of a cart – in fact probably this cart – on the way to East Oakhurst."

Victoria winced. "So you were! How did it happen? You never said."

"That's because I'm not really sure. One minute I was walking along confident I was heading for an archaeological dig the next someone had hit me over the head. The last thing I remember is a faint creaking. When I woke I was trussed up like a chicken…"

"Quiet." Robert pulled up the horse as the faint cry of a hunting horn and baying of hounds in full-cry ricocheted up the hill.

The horse stamped its foot. Harness jingling, it backed nervously until the tailboard of the cart was hanging over the side of the ridge.

"Jonathan, quick, grab its head." Biting his lip Robert held the horse on a tight rein.

Jonathan leapt out of the cart and ran to the front. He grabbed the bridle. Stroking the horse's muzzle he urged it forward. "Ssh… Ssh…" he soothed.

Trembling violently, the horse pulled the cart back on to the path. Jonathan glanced at Robert. "Have you the permit safe?"

"Yes – but it will not protect us here."

"Does it really matter?" Victoria said, her throat tight with tension.

"Of course, the permit is for the journey between Linhest and East Oakhurst."

The horn sounded again, louder and closer.

Robert cracked the whip. The horse leapt forward. Jonathan flung himself at the cart, grabbed hold of the nearest side and clung on, his feet dragging through the dust.

"Slow down," Victoria screamed reaching out for him.

Reluctantly, Robert pulled up the cart and peered down into the valley ready to crack his whip again should it be necessary… but the horsemen, their cloaks streaming out behind, were galloping towards a group of hounds that had brought down the tiring stag.

Chapter 22
The Death of a King

Victoria drew in an audible sigh of relief. "They've killed the deer."

Robert jumped down and went to the horse's head. Looking a little embarrassed he smiled sheepishly at Jonathan whose legs were trembling so violently he was having to hold on to the side of the cart for support. "Sorry," he said. "I panicked. Are you all right?"

Jonathan let go of the cart. "Yes," he said sounding surprised at finding he was still standing.

Robert glanced over the side of the ridge again. "Then if you're ready, we should move away. They might have had a kill but it would take only one rider to look up and see us."

Jonathan nodded.

Robert waited until he'd hauled himself painfully into the cart before climbing back on. He picked up the reins and gave them a quick flick. Tossing its head, the horse walked slowly towards a line of trees at the far end of the ridge.

At the entrance to the wood the horse hesitated then, stepping warily, walked in amongst the trees. Jonathan glanced around. A tingle ran down his spine. Everything was so familiar… there was the crunch of dead leaves on the track; then the eerie silence when they entered the copse of firs; the natural tunnel ahead.

He glanced at Victoria. "Well?" he asked.

A smile played over her lips. Her eyes sparkled. "We've been here before," she whispered.

"I know." Jonathan grinned. "Isn't it great when things go right?"

Relaxing a little they sat, enjoying the gentle swaying. From his seat on the box Robert whistled cheerfully. Almost imperceptibly a dappled light began filtering through the trees until the snatch of blue overhead turned into a wide expanse of clear blue sky.

"Jonathan!" Victoria stared down at the glen.

He laughed. "It's all right. I recognize it as well."

Without a change in pace the horse set off down the meandering track.

"This is *so* exciting." Victoria gazed at the familiar brakes of gorse. She nudged Jonathan as they drove past a sapling oak surrounded by a clump of brambles. "Do you remember that… and that? Oh, Jonathan, I can't believe it … we're actually here."

"This is it?" Startled, Robert jerked the reins and turned round. "*This* is your mysterious glen?"

They nodded, speechless as the memories flooded back. At the foot of the slope was the glade where, in the twenty-first century a monument stood recording the death of William Rufus – the Norman King they had seen only a few minutes ago hunting deer in the forest.

Clumps of bell heather covered the grassy slopes. Near the bottom was a large square of cropped grass that looked like a well-tended lawn. Yet they knew how deceptive that was because the turf was damp from the spring running through its centre. To its left damsel flies hovered above tufts of sedge growing through a patch of water-logged peat.

"Yes, Robert," Victoria said, finding her voice. A broad grin lit up her face. "Oh yes. This is the right place."

Caught up in her excitement Jonathan leaned forward and prodded Robert. "Can we stop right here?"

Robert frowned. "Yes… but should we not drive down to the bottom?"

"In a minute. There's something I want to check first." Jonathan jumped down. "Victoria, Ben try and remember where the monument was. I think it could have been there," he pointed at a slight dip at the foot of the slope.

"Possibly," said Ben shading his eyes.

"I'm not sure. Is it important," said Victoria.

"I believe it is," Jonathan said slowly. "Because if it was, then the car park would have been over there." He pointed.

"What will you do now?" said Robert watching him, his face unreadable.

Jonathan shrugged. "I really have no idea." He looked at Robert. "The only thing I do know – is that you should leave… now… while it's safe. Victoria, Ben, get down."

"Impossible... I cannot just drive away. It would be too dangerous. Someone might find you here."

"Robert, you don't have to worry about us," Jonathan said trying to sound more confident than he felt. "We're perfectly capable of looking after ourselves. Besides, there are loads of places we can hide if necessary. Please, just do what I ask."

Robert climbed down from the driver's box and lifted Victoria out of the cart. "I tell you Jonathan, I am not happy with this."

Victoria flung her arms around him. Standing on tiptoe she kissed his cheek. "You're so sweet. You know something, I am really going to miss you."

Ben and Jonathan clapped him on the back.

"Take care," said Jonathan.

Ben wrinkled his nose. "I wish we'd got our mobile phones on us. We could have taught you how to text. Then you could let us know when you got back to East Oakhurst."

"Ben... honestly!" Jonathan grinned at him. "Mobile phones don't exist... remember? There aren't any networks..."

"Mobile phones... text... networks. I do not understand. Please explain."

"No time." Victoria pushed him towards the cart. "And they're both talking nonsense." She glanced over her shoulder. "But Jonathan's right. You have got to go. Thank you... for everything. I don't know what we'd have done without you."

Robert smiled, a brief unhappy smile and hugged her. "Very well. Because you ask, Victoria, I will go." Releasing her he stepped back and called: "Farewell my friends. I will never forget any of you." He climbed up to the driver's box and gathered up the reins.

Ben and Victoria stepped aside. Jonathan grabbed the bridle. He hauled the horse around. When it faced back up the hill he let go and slapped the animal on its rump. "There you are," he said and moved out of the way.

Robert raised his whip in a salute.

"STOP!"

The two boys froze.

Victoria and Ben spun round. Fidgeting nervously in front of a tangle of brambles was the grey stallion they'd seen earlier in the day, its rider stern and grim-faced.

The King, thought Jonathan, dazed by this unexpected turn of events.

Clad in a dark blue tunic, his purple fur-lined cloak draped over the back of his horse, a gold circlet around his head confining his flaming, red hair, the King made an impressive figure.

He raised his bow and aimed the arrow at Robert. "Poachers…" he snarled. "I thought so when I saw you up on that ridge." He frowned. His fingers tightened around the string. "I think we have met before."

"Yes Sire, at East Oakhurst. You honoured my family when you attended my sister's wedding."

"Sir Henry Faversham's son… poaching? You have brought great shame on your parents. Think on it, boy. I

195

could have them imprisoned with you… or worse."

The colour drained from Robert's face. "My L… Lord."

William Rufus smiled; a cruel smile. "Have no fear. I am merciful. Your trial and execution will be punishment enough for your unfortunate parents."

The stallion pawed the ground. Exclaiming angrily he wheeled it around in a complete circle until it had settled again. "You," he pointed the arrow momentarily at Jonathan, "…and you and you…," the arrow swung round in a semi-circle taking in Victoria and Ben, "… get back in that cart."

Jonathan looked at him, wondering whether to risk startling the horse. It was so nervous it wouldn't take much to panic it, he thought.

As though reading his mind the King added: "Do not do anything foolish or I will let loose the arrow."

There was a long, tense silence. Jonathan, Victoria and Ben stared, fascinated, at the arrow once again aimed at Robert. Although the hand holding the bow seemed quite steady they could see that the string was quivering.

"Come on you two," Jonathan said sensing the very real danger they were in.

"Very wise." The King curled his lip. "When you are…"

They never discovered what he was going to say because at that moment an arrow sped past them, its flight level and direct.

The King grunted and sagged in the saddle, an arrowhead embedded deep in his chest.

Whinnying, the powerful stallion reared, nostrils flaring it pawed the air with its front hooves. It was like a slow-motion movie, Jonathan thought watching as the rider slithered from the saddle. As the King's body rolled down the slope a shrill scream broke the silence.

Spooked, the stallion reared again, turned and bolted, reins flapping, the stirrups pounding its flanks.

A second scream ended in a sob.

Victoria was staring at the King, her mouth open, ashen-faced.

"Stop it," Jonathan ordered. He stepped between her and the body and grabbed her shoulders, shaking her. "Stop it. Do you want the rest of the hunt to hear?"

She hiccupped. Her legs buckled. He caught her and held her tight. Over her head his eyes met Robert's. "Go," he said. "Don't argue. We'll be all right. Just go."

Robert opened his mouth, closed it again, shook his head and urged the old horse forward.

"Better now?" Jonathan patted the top of Victoria's head – her face still buried in his chest.

She glanced up, her cheeks tear-stained and streaked. "Sorry… I'm so sorry. Is he really dead?"

"Have a look if you don't believe it."

Victoria peered round him. Her expression turned to one of bewilderment. "Where… what have you done with him?"

Jonathan stared. "Done with him? Nothing, there

197

hasn't been time… damn – now it's beginning to rain."
He looked across the glen and stiffened.

In a nearby car park a young woman was climbing out of a blue mini.

She waved.

Jonathan let out a long soft breath. Suddenly everything fell into place. "Ben, Victoria," he said urgently. "Do you trust me?"

"Of course," Ben sounded puzzled.

The woman was running up the path.

"Then listen… carefully," he said. "This is important… you must agree with whatever I say – will you promise me that?"

Chapter 23
The Sun, Moon and Stars

Three figures emerged from the drizzle. Sylvene switched on the wipers and peered through the windscreen. They looked as though they had come from a different time… a time long ago. The girl was wearing a long dress. Her hair was hidden by a scarf or… Sylvene drew in her breath… a wimple? She gripped the steering wheel and turned her attention on the boys. Both were wearing short tunics. Cloaks hung from their shoulders.

Sylvene slumped in the seat with relief. Unless she was mistaken the clothes belonged to the Norman period. It must be them. Her hand shaking a little she wrenched opened the door, slid her long legs out and ran to the Rufus Stone.

Victoria was the first to reach her. Sylvene flung her arms around her and kissed her damp cheek. "Thank goodness… you're safe."

"Don't," said Victoria wriggling free. "People are watching."

Disappointed, Sylvene stepped back. "I don't think so. They're far too busy sheltering from this rain. But if it worries you I'll stop."

"Jonathan and Ben can see. Look how they're smirking. Sylvene, did you know we'd get back today?

How long have you been waiting?"

Sylvene blinked at the rapid questions. "No I didn't and ... not long. In fact Victoria I haven't been waiting as you put it. We were talking to each other only a few minutes ago while looking at the Rufus Stone."

"You haven't been waiting?" Victoria frowned, puzzled.

"What's the matter?" Jonathan said, coming closer and putting his arm around her shoulder.

"I think Sylvene believes we haven't been away. How can that be possible? Tell her Jonathan. Tell her it isn't true. We've been gone ages."

"Er... Victoria... I didn't say you haven't been away. No wait... let me explain." Sylvene smiled at them – a strange fixed smile.

"Perhaps you should – explain I mean," Jonathan said his expression grave. "Someone needs to. It might as well be you."

Sylvene shot him an uncertain glance. "All right, but you have to promise to be patient. It's a complicated story. A story involving the perpetual struggle between good and evil and interwoven with time-travel and loss."

"Oh, we'll be patient," said Jonathan.

Victoria and Ben nodded.

"Thank you... the question as always is where to begin?"

"Obviously with the time-travel," Jonathan interrupted.

"Very well." Sylvene sounded uneasy. "Time-travel has the capacity to distort time – which can be confusing."

"What's today's date?" Jonathan said suddenly.

"The second of August."

"Are you saying that all the time we were in Norman England you've been sitting in your car, waiting for the rain to stop?" Ben said.

Sylvene clapped her hands. "Norman England… So I was right… you had to go back to Norman England."

"That's not what I asked."

She frowned. "There's no need to be so belligerent Ben… but yes… you're right.

"We drove into the car park just after twelve o'clock. While you three were looking at the monument I went back to the car to get out of the rain. I must have been waiting for you for," Sylvene glanced at her wristwatch, "oh, I don't know… about fifteen minutes."

"That's not what I remember," Victoria whispered in Jonathan's ear.

"Really?" Sylvene sounded offended. She tapped the face of her watch. "Look… doesn't it say half past twelve on the 2nd August – that's the anniversary of the death of William Rufus. And you'll find the picnic in the boot. Don't just take my word for it – check the basket and ask one of the tourists what date it is."

"Now who's being belligerent?" Ben said.

"No I'm not I…"

"It's all right we believe you. Besides, they'd think we were mad." Jonathan shot a quick frown at Ben. At the same time he squeezed Victoria's shoulders warningly. "Sylvene, there's loads to tell you. Some of it's pretty strange. Do you know we actually saw the King being killed?"

"Oh yes… it was horrible." Victoria shivered.

"My dear," Sylvene stepped closer. "How awful… I can imagine…"

"Can you Sylvene? Can you really imagine?" An inflexible note had crept into Jonathan's voice. He stepped in front of the young woman, his expression grim. "You knew what was going to happen, didn't you?"

"Me?"

"Yes. You let us go back to Norman England without warning us…"

"Can I interrupt and say how great you all look?"

Jonathan scowled but decided to ignore the comment. "As I was saying, you let us go back without any warning…"

Victoria prodded him in the back.

"What?"

"It's stopped raining. Wouldn't it be a good idea to find somewhere less conspicuous to have this talk?"

"Yes, people are beginning to look," Sylvene said. She wrinkled her forehead. "I don't think there's anything to worry about what Victoria's wearing. Lots of girls wear long dresses these days. But those tunics," she shook her head. "That's different. I've never seen anyone dressed like that."

"I have." Victoria giggled nervously. "But only in a play."

"Exactly," said Sylvene.

"Let's go to the car," said Jonathan.

Sylvene shook her head. "No, far too cramped. I've got a better idea. Over there." She pointed at a copse of young oaks growing some distance from the road on the west side of the glade. "It's quiet and very few people bother to go that far away from the monument."

"That's true," said Jonathan. "Okay… let's go there."

Sylvene smiled as she set off across the glade, picking her way carefully around the worst of the boggy patches. The others almost seemed to relish squelching through the sodden mud and slime.

At the edge of the copse Victoria grimaced and stopped. She pulled at the damp skirt flapping unpleasantly against her legs.

Sylvene half-turned, one hand raised to push aside a low hanging branch in her way. "Try and keep up," she called impatiently.

Jonathan slowed, deliberately. "Why? What's the hurry?"

"There isn't one. I'm just anxious to hear everything. What about in here? It's private. There's no one around. But say if you don't like it. We can always find another place."

"No… this will do. It's not too from the road. I like being able to… to…" Catching sight of Sylvene's quizzical expression Jonathan floundered for a moment before continuing in a rush: "…to see the cars and coaches. They're a great reminder we're really back."

Sylvene stiffened. Then she smiled and released the branch. "So be it. Sit down. The ground's quite dry." She stood in front of them, waiting until all the wriggling and restlessness had stopped before leaning forward, her face eager. "Jonathan, what were you saying just... oh, for heaven's sake Victoria, what's wrong now?"

"Someone's watching us – over there." Victoria pointed in the direction of a brake of gorse on the far side of the road.

"Don't be so silly." Sylvene didn't even bother to look around. "If there was anyone there it was probably a hiker – more likely it was your imagination. I can't see anyone. Now, Jonathan, what were you saying?"

"I did Ben, I did," Victoria whispered. "There was somebody standing in that gap. He had a hood over his head so I couldn't see his face but I *know* he was watching us."

Jonathan met Sylvene's gaze without flinching. "I wanted you to understand how awful it was when we realised what had happened; when we were wandering around the twelfth century with no idea how we'd got there, or why we were there; or how we were going to get back. Yet you knew what was going to happen, didn't you Sylvene? You must have known before you brought us to the New Forest. So why didn't you tell us? You could have warned us, explained what was going on."

Victoria nudged Ben. "That man's still there," she hissed. "I can see him. He's watching us. No don't look now. Take your time, slowly... slowly."

Ben turned sideways, grabbed a long stem of grass, broke it off and proceeded to chew the stalk.

"Well? Did you see him?"

He nodded.

"That settles it… Sylvene…"

"Not now, Victoria." Sylvene held up her hand. "Jonathan – what are you trying to say?"

"Isn't it obvious? I'm trying to show you how it looks to us."

"What is 'it'?"

"Sylvene, you're not stupid. You know exactly what I mean. You let us go back through time without any warning. What I don't understand is having done that, why did you show yourself to Victoria in the mirror? That was the obvious give away. If you hadn't done that we'd probably never have guessed you were involved."

"If I hadn't done that you'd probably still be in Norman England."

"Would we?"

"Oh yes. Trust me. You were getting nowhere. Without my help the three of you would have been trapped in the twelfth century for the rest of your life."

"Ben…" Victoria clutched his arm. "There are more of them… look. They're all watching us." She shivered. "I don't like it. What's happening?"

"But why Sylvene? You still haven't told us *why* you sent us there?

Sylvene stared at Jonathan. "Are you telling me you haven't guessed? Jonathan, Jonathan, you disappoint me. It's really quite simple. I need the Sun."

Startled, Ben and Victoria glanced at her.

"What's that?" asked Ben.

"Don't interrupt, Ben. Aeons ago four Talismans were forged and given to four human families on the orders of the Seigneurs of the five universes.

"Today a danger threatens Earth. A danger so great it was ordered that the four Talismans be brought together. Only then could the forces of evil be defeated."

"That's why the Sun had to be reunited with the Moon and Stars?"

She nodded. "Yes, Jonathan. Without it evil will control your universe. And that is why I sent you into the twelfth century."

"If you knew where it was why didn't you go and get it yourself?" demanded Victoria.

"I knew the date when it was lost and the place where the Guardian had lived. But I didn't know where it had been hidden. Besides, if I had found it what good would it have been? I still wouldn't have been able to bring it back with me. Only the Guardians of the Moon and Stars could do that."

"Only the Guardians… I don't understand… why not you? And why didn't you tell us what you wanted us to do?" said Ben.

"Would you have believed me?"

"Probably not," he said slowly.

There was a long pause before Victoria said: "You haven't explained why you wouldn't have been able to bring the Sun back."

"Because child when the four Talismans were crafted

it was deemed only humans should look after them. That is why the Gleeman…"

There was a shocked gasp.

Sylvene smiled a strange, ironic smile. "Oh yes, the Gleeman… I learned all about the Gleeman when I started my quest for the Sun. When I learned he was visiting East Oakhurst I knew it was time to warn you even though, like me, he needed you to carry the Sun back to the twenty-first century. Once here his intention was to give the Talisman to the young man he had chosen to be the new Guardian; a young man completely in his power. That is why he did you no harm."

"What about you? What do you propose to do with the Sun?" Jonathan said very quietly.

Sylvene smiled, but the smile couldn't disguise a growing coldness in her eyes. "I, too, have found a human willing to be the new Guardian of the Sun. An honest, intelligent young man, one ready to fight the forces of evil alongside you should it become necessary." She turned her smile on Victoria. "My dear, I apologise. You were right. Someone is watching us." She stood up and beckoned. "Richard, come over here. I want you to meet the Guardians."

Victoria's fingernails dug deep into Ben's arms as a hooded figure rose out of the shadows of the gorse and walked slowly across the road.

"Ouch. Stop it, Victoria. That hurts." Ben shook himself free.

"Who is he?" Victoria whispered staring at the

burning eyes in the gaunt face.

"A young man willing to face danger. Give him the Sun, Jonathan."

"No!"

Sylvene drew herself up to her full height. "What did you say?"

Jonathan swallowed. "No." Victoria began shivering. He looked across at her with concern. "What is it?"

"There are more." Her voice was tight with fear. "Lot's more… look…"

Jonathan and Ben sprang to their feet. Grabbing her arms they pulled Victoria up and dragged her into the trees away from the shadowy figures now slithering out of the gorse.

"It is useless trying to escape." A cruel smile shaped Sylvene's lips. "Besides, why would you want to? These are friends… my friends. My friends should be your friends. All they want to do is protect the Talismans and the Guardians." Her voice hardened. "And Richard *will* become one of those Guardians – whatever you think. Now give him the Sun, Jonathan."

Jonathan stood quite still. "No, Sylvene." He gasped in alarm as Victoria ducked out from under his arm and tried to grab her but was too late.

Skidding to a stop in front of Sylvene but just out of her reach she turned back to him as she fumbled at the neck of her dress. "Quickly, get out the Talismans…"

The air of confidence faded. Doubt flickered in Sylvene's eyes as Victoria held up the Moon. Behind

Sylvene a dense, impenetrable mist began to envelop some of the approaching figures.

Sylvene's gaze hardened. Glancing at Ben and Jonathan who were still struggling to find their Talismans she raised her arm. At once their eyes glazed over.

"Help me," Victoria screamed as her hand began shaking violently.

Neither boy moved. Both seemed oblivious to the mass creeping across the grass, unhindered, towards her.

The Moon began rocking backwards and forwards in her hand. Victoria groaned. An unseen force was dragging the Talisman from her grasp. Sylvene had won. She was going to fail...

Just as the thought swept over her a crack of thunder shattered the silence.

Behind her Jonathan blinked and rubbed his eyes. Through a thick haze he heard the muffled scream. A wave of fear swept over him. He pushed Ben forward and staggered after him. Above them the blue sky vanished beneath a monstrous bank of black clouds. Another crack of thunder rolled around the glade.

Clutching each other all three held up their Talismans, Victoria the Moon, Ben his Star, Jonathan his Star and the Sun.

A blinding flash of lightning struck the ground immediately in front of Sylvene. She backed away. A sudden gust of wind stirred the dead leaves around her feet. It gathered speed and, roaring loudly, rushed forward, twisting and turning, a miniature tornado collecting everything in its path. Darkness descended, a pervading darkness, a darkness filled with terrified muffled cries.

Four golden rays ripped apart the clouds. A dazzling light floated down and surrounded the Guardians, creating an impenetrable fence. Outside the fence sparks flew into the sky. Lightning flashed. Thunder rolled.

Jonathan, Victoria and Ben watched, horrified, as a barrage of splinters flew at the swirling mass still approaching. The man, Richard, flung up his left arm. Covering his eyes he ducked under a branch of a tree. But the others were trapped in their own hiding place with nowhere to go. Thrashing backwards and forwards, they fought vainly, trying to evade the gleaming shards.

The wind was now a raging vortex. It sliced through the mist its tendrils endlessly searching. First one shadowy figure was flung into the open and whirled into the sky, then another, and another. The onslaught continued until all that remained were a few strands of mist floating above the grass. The last threads blew away. For a long moment the stream of light blazed white - then vanished.

Stunned, Jonathan, Victoria and Ben stared. Only two other people remained – Sylvene and Richard. Once they had appeared invincible. Now they were mere relics of a defeated force.

A deep chuckle broke the tense silence.

Everyone looked around.

The Gleeman was leaning against a tree, watching.

He straightened up and smiled at Jonathan, Victoria and Ben. "Well done." His voice resonated with warmth and pride.

With a defiant glare at the newcomer, Sylvene and Richard walked towards the road and vanished.

Chapter 24
Explanations

Jonathan and Ben grinned at him inanely. Victoria stared at the empty road. Sensing her confusion the Gleeman walked past the boys and placed his hand on her shoulder. "What is it my child?"

She turned to him, her distress gradually replaced by a puzzled look. "I don't understand."

"What don't you understand?"

"Anything – everything Sylvene said – the Seigneurs, Guardians – none of it made any sense."

The Gleeman sighed. "Much of what she told you is true, but she manipulated it to fit her own needs. There are five universes. Each is protected by a Seigneur."

Ben and Jonathan moved closer.

"Is our universe one of them?" said Jonathan.

The Gleeman nodded.

"How can there be so many?" Ben said, bewildered.

"Why should there not be other universes?"

"I don't know… we're finding out more about space all the time. Perhaps we'll find another one soon," said Ben.

"Where do the 'Seigneurs' come in?" Victoria asked.

The Gleeman turned back to her. "They created the four Talismans before the beginning of time… time, that is, in your universe… to protect Earth from the forces of evil. Sylvene is the servant of those forces. She was sent to steal the Talismans."

"Why?" said Ben.

"Her masters intended to seize control of your planet. Oh, not openly. No one would see them working yet their evil would reach out its long tentacles and slowly stifle all that was good, leaving only misery and pain in their wake."

Victoria shivered. "If Sylvene is their servant, why did she give up so easily when we told her she couldn't have the Talismans?"

"She has not given up, Victoria. She would not dare to. Her orders were to return with the Talismans and that is what she must do. She had hoped to succeed through deception and trickery. This failure will have angered her masters. She will not risk doing that again. She will return stronger and more determined."

"You think she will return?" said Jonathan, frowning. "Surely not? We'd never let her take us in again."

"Undoubtedly she will return; not in the guise that you know her. No, if you see the Sylvene you know it will be because she wants you to see her. From now on you must never lower your guard. View everyone you meet with suspicion. Trust nobody…"

"Nobody? What about you?" Ben said quickly. "Can we trust you?"

The Gleeman smiled sadly. "You learn fast, my boy. Let us first talk. Afterwards you shall tell me whether or not you can trust me. My greatest fear, when you returned to your time, was that you would concede to Sylvene's demands. I am glad I was proved wrong. Tell me, what made you decide to refuse to do what she asked?"

"Jonathan," Victoria and Ben said, immediately.

The Gleeman glanced at Jonathan, a quizzical question in his eyes.

Jonathan reddened. "This is going to sound stupid but I started to have doubts about Sylvene as soon as I realised we'd gone back in time. Then, when she showed herself to Victoria I just knew we shouldn't trust her. A friend, a real friend, wouldn't have sent us into danger without some kind of warning. There was also the way she kept insisting we should give the Sun to this Richard... That reminds me, why couldn't she go back for it? You obviously could."

The Gleeman smiled. "Of course she could have gone back. Like me, she can travel through time. But she was right. If she had found the Sun she would still have needed you there. Only the chosen few... the Guardians... can handle the Talismans."

Ben stared at him, wide-eyed. "That means you..."

The Gleeman nodded. "Yes, Ben. If you tried to give me your Star I would not be able to take it. In fact, although I knew where the Sun was..."

"How did you know?" Ben said.

"Simple, when each Talisman was created it was I whom the Seigneurs entrusted with the task of protecting them. Every minute of every day I have known where each one was.

"The three of you have discovered where there is great good there is also great evil; but you had to learn it at great personal risk. Sadly, there are still too many of your people who would use the Talismans for evil purposes. That is why the Sun, the Moon and the Stars have to be protected by innocence. It is why my masters chose children from four families to shelter them. A child from each was given a Talisman and charged to hand it to their eldest child when he or she reached the age of ten. This worked smoothly until Edgar died."

"Couldn't you have found another family to take care of the Sun after he died?" Jonathan asked.

"I could have, but there was no need. The Moon and Stars were following their chosen paths through the centuries. I, as Protector of the Talismans, knew where Edgar had hidden the Sun. The balance was maintained... until Sylvene was sent to find all four Talismans by her Masters."

Jonathan, Victoria and Ben stared at him in silence. Seeing their serious faces the Gleeman relaxed a little. "Don't look so worried."

"But you said Sylvene would probably try again," said Victoria.

"Not probably – she will. But the time for that is not yet upon us. Let me say how proud I am of your efforts. I am confident that you will be able to prevent any further attempts with my help. Luckily Sylvene does not know about me..."

"Oh, but she does," Jonathan said.

The Gleeman raised an incredulous eyebrow. "What makes you say that?"

"She warned Victoria about you."

"He's right. When she showed herself to me in Adela's hand mirror she told me we had to be careful of someone called the Gleeman."

"The thing is we didn't even know who or what the Gleeman was until we heard one of the children call you by that name at the wedding," said Ben.

The Gleeman smiled. "I remember. That is why you looked so shocked." He grew serious again. "If Sylvene knows about me I must warn the Seigneurs to expect a renewed onslaught of evil."

Taking a deep breath Victoria faced the Gleeman. "What do you want us to do?" she asked proudly.

The Gleeman smiled at her. "Nothing! For the moment you have done enough." He reached out to her. "Trust me, child. When you need me I will be there."

"Were you in the forest when the king was killed?" Ben asked unexpectedly.

"Yes. I was never far from your side from the moment you arrived in the New Forest."

"Did you see who shot him?"

The Gleeman studied his fingernails for a moment. When he looked up, his expression was sombre, his eyes darkening. "I did."

"I thought so."

The twinkle returned to the man's eyes at Ben's smug and self-satisfied expression.

"What are you talking about?" demanded Victoria.

"The Gleeman shot the King."

"He did what?"

"You heard."

The Gleeman nodded. "I had to. If I hadn't killed him Robert would have been executed and so, no doubt, would you. When I heard his challenge I put an arrow in my bow and let it fly… and… well you know the rest."

"What about Robert? What happened to him? Did he get home safely?" Jonathan said.

"He did. And he married the following year. His parents chose his bride wisely. When Robert inherited the estate he and his wife ruled it with care and kindness. Jonathan, you are the eldest, albeit only by a few weeks, but nonetheless you are the eldest. I give the Sun into your charge."

"Me?"

"Yes, you for the eldest must always shoulder much of the responsibility. Now, I must leave. You will be able to find your way home."

It was a statement, not a question.

They nodded. He turned, but stopped as Victoria caught his sleeve. "Before you go," she said, "please can you tell me what the rings on the back of my Talisman mean?"

The Gleeman hugged her. "Why, they link the heavenly bodies – the suns, moons and stars in every universe. Now I must go and tell my masters all that has happened."

A shaft of bright sunlight lit up their surroundings blinding each of them. It vanished as quickly as it had come.

Blinking, they looked around.

There was no one nearby.

"I didn't imagine it, did I? There was someone called the 'Gleeman' here a moment ago, wasn't there?" said Ben.

"No, you didn't imagine it," said Victoria. "What I want to know was what did that bit about Jonathan and responsibility mean?"

"I guess it means I'm in charge." Jonathan ducked as Victoria flung a handful of soggy leaves at him. "And if I'm in charge then I say – let's go home."